ONCE YOU GO BACK

ONCE YOU GO BACK

Douglas A. Martin

Seven Stories Press
NEW YORK

Seven Stories Press
140 Watts Street
New York, NY 10013
www.sevenstories.com

In Canada: Publishers Group Canada, 559 College Street, Suite 402, Toronto, ON M6G 1A9

In the UK: Turnaround Publisher Services Ltd., Unit 3, Olympia Trading Estate, Coburg Road, Wood Green, London N22 6TZ

In Australia: Palgrave Macmillan, 15–19 Claremont Street, South Yarra, VIC 3141

College professors may order examination copies of Seven Stories Press titles for a free six-month trial period. To order, visit www.sevenstories.com/textbook or send a fax on school letterhead to (212) 226-1411.

Book design by Jon Gilbert

Library of Congress Cataloging-in-Publication Data

Martin, Douglas A.
 Once you go back / Douglas A. Martin. -- 1st ed.
     p. cm.
 ISBN 978-1-58322-878-4 (pbk.)
 1. Broken homes--Fiction. 2. Problem families--Fiction. 3. Brothers and sisters--Fiction. 4. Stepfathers--Fiction. 5. Gay teenagers--Fiction. I. Title.
 PS3563.A72355O53 2009
 813´.54--dc22

                                        2008038724

Printed in the United States of America

9 8 7 6 5 4 3 2 1

Leoma Katherine Benseman,
February 25, 1925–August 4, 1999

Arthur Wayland Krick,
April 8, 1921–March 17, 2007

ꝏꝏꝏꝏꝏꝏ

To escape from horror bury yourself in it.
JEAN GENET

1

A Tall One

PRETEND YOU ARE MY SISTER. There are silos in the distance, in the sky above the house out in the country, where our real dad's parents live. Our noses run from the wind that turns our skin red. We are where he was raised as a boy, in a house of two stories. It is before he is taken away. The fields are full. Inside, I hide in a small closet under the staircase for the coats, calling this my room. Skyrockets in flight, afternoon delight, a song on the radio. It drifts through the house, a low, lilting melody. The man then our grandfather sits in a stuffed armchair, yellow, resting. The air outside is cold but bright and clear. You can't find me. My lips pursed in a hum. He once chased us with his hands.

You are bound not to remember much of this, like later there will be things you'll try not to. But there was him, and there were others who came after him. One is the tallest man ever, barely fitting into the new house that's an apartment in a brick triplex he is so tall. He'd have to duck to get inside the door the ceilings are so low. He is almost as skinny as me, though. Our mom won't marry this one, when she marries again. It's too soon after our real dad left, our last names still beginning with almost the end of the alphabet. Every time he came over, that one lifted me up, and I'd perch on his shoulders, touching the ceiling. He'd ride me around the house like this. He's sick, always, from when we first know him, and later our mom will cry when he does die. He must have been one of those men, even back then. There's always been something wrong with him. He'd be the last man she invites into our house for a while. Then she goes quiet, not knowing what to say in the wake of his death. She'd reached out, to him, and then there was a period of none.

2

The Dark

OUR MOM TELLS STORIES of me climbing out of my own crib, how unbelievable I was at that age, the way I would use the chest of drawers beside the crib to escape, how I'd hoist myself up onto the top, get out of the crib onto the dresser, then making my way down to the floor by stepping off into drawers below me I'd pull out, like a ladder under me, slowly, with my toes, making my way down until I was close enough to the floor to let myself fall the rest of the way without then getting hurt. That dresser could have toppled over onto me, she says. You don't think of such things. Some nights she'd come look for me in my crib and I'd be gone, gotten out of the house. She'd find me sitting there on the front porch.

When her bed is empty again, except for her, there's room enough for me. Some nights it's just too much trouble to make me leave. She'll let me stay there, or she'll wait until I fall asleep and then carry me back to my bed. Some nights she asks me what I'm doing, when I'm trying to move into the dark room, where she's been quietly sleeping. I'm afraid of the dark, bumps in the house, eyes bolting open, while you are dreaming. I want nothing else too bad to happen. In the room we share, the streetlight outside a window fizzles, shorts. At times, sheer limbs of illumination peek through, until it then goes off again. I'd like all the lights in the house left on at night.

I know I'm somewhere I don't belong. You don't remember being anywhere else, ever, but I do. What we mean to each other becomes tighter the longer we go without anyone else. Where you go when you go away is up north. They are all still up there.

In the middle of the night, I want to know there are still other bodies in the house. I want to be assured, not left alone. There's nothing worse, I think, than to see just the dark when you open your eyes.

I'm old enough to walk in my blue socks. I advance across the carpet carefully, with my feet like testing waters. The blood in the shells of my ears quickens. I want her to cover me up, to tuck me in. She's in her room all alone, and I can't fall asleep for worrying about her, you. I'm too hot in my pajamas. From the doorway, the door to her room she some nights will leave open, I watch her breathing, her sky nightgown rise and fall, satin light across her pale chest in shadows.

By heart, I know the way there past the fish tank, how the cold heat of its lamp over the water cuts through to them that swim, all, never sleep either, fin through the night. There's one other light I make her promise to not turn out, left on in the small square of the bathroom above the mirror, even after she's gone to bed. Some nights she does. It's a different dark then.

If some man takes us to the zoo, he might one day become our new dad. If I don't make a sound climbing up, don't place too much of my weight down on the end of her bed all at once, our mom might not wake, might not even know I'm there, and then I won't have to go back to my own bed. I stand there quietly, move closer, get warmer. I keep moving, but keeping quiet, making a way along the wall. Some nights instead I'll go climbing up the bunk ladder to the top one and try to wedge myself between my sister's sleeping body and the wall. Pretend you are her. Since my bed is the bottom one, I always think if anyone breaks into the house, I'll be the first one found. Close to the ceiling, I watch you breathing.

OUR MOM SITS ALONE at the kitchen table, trying to balance the checkbook, trying to make the money last, so little is being put into the account. We have to eat. She has to feed us. One day she'll have a better, bigger house, but she can't know that yet. One day you'll be able to marry a man like the next one she finds. She has to try and get some sleep before getting up early to go back to work the next morning. She's working a double tomorrow. She'll have to find someone to watch us. She can't think about what's going on in her heart right now. She has to feed us. We were surviving, and that's the important thing. That's all there is. We could have the rest of her food, if we were still hungry.

We all know it's the absence of someone like a real dad in our lives that creates this constant desperation. It's not really our house. We're just renting it. It's not even really a house. We could be asked to go at any time. She reminds us constantly of that. What could we do to help her? We'd have to forget about him, our dad. He wasn't coming back. So that memory of his hand around my ankle, washing me as an infant, as I smile, goes from the mind and only stays in a picture hidden. If she no longer has him to fall back on, why should we. We'd soon see how much better it is without someone like him in that small apartment. She has us. We're enough for her, she says. And she had her job at the hospital.

Later, I'll study the point in the picture where his arm has crept into the frame. Then I know what his arm looks like. I believe you could tell a lot by that. If you weren't looking closely, you would never even notice his arm was right there all along. Sometimes he wore a uniform, I know. He must have, because he was in the Air Force, but I'd remember him only in jeans and a white T-shirt that one day out in the country. Later on in life, I'll decide the suit was part of the problem, the same one you'll later put on. It was nothing to do with me, or the way I might have looked at him wrong, how we both might have looked to him. He had to run away, and he had to return to that place, out in the country in the North, back to his mother and father's farm, the horses there, breathing a final sigh of relief, having left it all behind, making it. I know once he left I never grabbed desperately at him.

SHE MAKES US GET INTO the closet with a mattress. The tornado, for which there's been a warning, actually comes very close, rips up a tree right in our front yard. It will go flying by while we are huddled up all in that same place together, our mom crying, telling us to remember whatever happens she loves us. It scares us when she tells us how we have to be now. Then we'd start crying too, just like her, listening as we believe we hear another one in our yard being pulled up by its roots, believe we hear the tree land in the road, branches snapped off every which way.

THE WHITE STREETLIGHT WILL cast a grayish shade through the one window high up in the room I shared with you. Some nights I do still lie there and think about our dad. It doesn't matter now. He couldn't see us anyway. Nobody was going to look in that window without a curtain and see us. The dark swallowed you in sleep, and that's when sometimes I would still dream about him. In the middle of the night, I'd get up to crawl into her bed again. Some nights I'd try to just curl at the foot, because then there was less of a chance of waking her up. If I could just fall asleep beside her, then she could carry me back to my own bed, gently placing me back down.

I have an overactive imagination, because I'm dreaming of dying every night. One night I dream our mom gone, too. Or she's sitting at the kitchen table with people who are already dead. I am scared at night below you in the bed, scared of where I'll go if I go to sleep.

The monkeys with wings on the TV scare you. The one thing I can't wait for each year is when the color in the movie changes, when it all takes that turn for the better and brighter, the black and white and gray becoming a whole other spectrum. At night, the best was when you have a good dream. That's when everything feels like it can change, when everything appears so alive suddenly then, and things really start to happen.

3

Kinder

THE IDEA OF CAMOUFLAGE appeals to me, the way that animals learn to blend into their surroundings. Sitting at the round table, I'm the only boy at mine. I try not to notice my obvious preferences too much. I'm learning to write my name. I sit next to a Chinese girl the other boys and even the prettier girls avoid getting too close to. I'll wear home the bunny ears we made for Easter, the same basic design we use during Thanksgiving to make what our teacher calls our headdresses. A single feather would be cut out of our choice of paper, poke up tall at the back of our heads, after being stapled to another band of paper looped around, like the base of a crown, slipping down to rest behind our ears. When I come home, you'll want one, too.

At recess, they line up to buy extra milks. You are supposed to bring your supply money tomorrow, but these are the little expenses our mother can't afford without help from our dad, who's not helping us. She'll remind us that he made his decision. If he ever wanted to see us again, he'd never be able to, because he owed us too much money. That house in the country, the one with a field I can barely remember now, becomes in my mind what's behind a piece of white paper. Don't think about it. You don't need a picture to color in, lines already clearly demarcated for us. Just imagine. Draw your own. Draw white on white, the moon with a white crayon. You were at home being watched by I don't know who. There wasn't a hazel crayon, the color of his and your eyes. You don't have the same color as me and our mom, blue, mixed with some gray. Our mom had to assure you yours were just as pretty. They were unique. I've started to draw the picture of our family without him there, though I wouldn't get far with my representation of the truth without someone pointing out this or that, accusing me of doing it wrong. There's only one big body in my picture. Now hurry up and finish. The teacher says it's the end of the day. There's no time to try to fit in the woman who pops up in my mind, stern, who must have been I see our grandmother on his side. It was harder to remember them the less you saw them. The fact that he couldn't handle something about us is like a scab I can't stop picking at, never going to heal. Once we've forgotten about it, it would be brought to our attention by someone else. Then it would start hurting again.

It's been so long past a real photograph would by now have long begun to pull apart into its initial components, the backing coming away from the layer developed over, and traces in between not to be touched, because they were chemicals, and it was dangerous.

You snored lightly above me in the dark. No more fights in the house woke us up. Isn't that better. Wasn't that a relief. We'd both come running to see what was happening, the nights she'd get home from work late because he wasn't going in to work again this week. He's too drunk for work. He was going to have to call in sick. They were going to get rid of him, if he keeps on. I tried from my bed to keep track of the bodies as they shifted back and forth before the crack left in our bedroom door. Since he left the last time, we still hadn't heard from him.

Our mom tells me it could have been worse, when I complain about my name. I could have been named what he wanted to name me. Back at school, we were still learning to write it. When you look it up in a book, or the teacher does it for you, it means dark sea. Our dad would say that up in Heaven Jesus had a big book that he'd write down every thing we had done in. It was how he kept track of whether you were good or bad, if you were going to get to join him again once you died. But I'd learned to start picking up on the contradictions. Just as often, God had a big book up in Heaven with everyone's name written down in it already, everyone who was going to go there. This was what we were told when we began to panic. It was never too late, see, as he tried to reason his way out of the conflicting stories. One was God, and the other was his son, Jesus. Like he and the next man in the house would be two different men, don't get them confused. All that mattered is he was watching us. He made you feel a certain way, running after you, suddenly grabbing you, pulling you up into the air in his arms. But once he went away, all of that goes away, too. At school I swing when it's recess. Boys don't run around the way I do. I'm no good at the games they play. You'd start next year.

They play a game together where everyone hangs out across from each other in the center of the monkey bars, trying to pull each other down, to make each other fall by wrapping your legs around someone. Who could hang by their arms the longest would be the winner. The grass leaves tracks of green, its streaks on the knees of my jeans. My only pair. The size I wear is slim. Try not to ruin them. The size I wear is slim. Husky is the size other boys fit into. They have better ones, but mine will last longer. They have to, all year or more. She'd buy them a couple of sizes too long, hem them up for now. When I've grown a couple of inches, our mom could then take out the seams.

At first I couldn't wait to start going there. I thought it could make everything change somehow. School would take my mind off the emptiness of the house. Nobody there would have to see where we come from, either, to know, and I had to try to stop being so attached to our mom and you.

The boys played rough, but they're just playing with each

other, just playing like their older brothers and their fathers. The girls at school gravitate together, at lunch bringing their chocolate milk money. Ours would be reduced. You were glad at the end of the day when I got home.

OUR GRANDFATHER WOULD teach me to look both ways, do it twice, look both ways again, before crossing the road. Just to make sure. Holding my hand. They were down visiting from up north, helping our mom, to give her a break from us kids. They could help her buy some things that we'd been needing around the house. But they couldn't stay forever.

We were crossing a busy intersection. I feel nervous about holding his hand. But I never get to see him, my grandfather. Usually I would stand on the steps outside after everyone has already gone on the bus or been picked up by their parents who stay home. Our mom would be there as soon as she could get off work. I think I can walk home. Why can't I just walk home. Our house was just a road or two away from the school.

Our mom can't believe we have to already have real notebook paper, in the second grade already, where I don't know what a paragraph is.

She'd be there just as soon as she could. All day long now I couldn't wait for the bell to ring, for the day to be over. Then I don't want anyone to see how I wait for her. Then she'll show up to school in her uniform.

One day I say I have an appointment, tell the teacher that I have to leave school early. I have to go see the principal, who wants to know why I don't have a note. My mom is going to be waiting outside to pick me up, he's going to make me miss her, and I have my appointment. I'm crying, telling him how it's going to be his fault. I have to go back to class, because it's the rule, but I just go outside, instead. I start walking, after looking around, from the front steps. The school is close. There are cars, but I don't have to go too far. Our grandmother is staying behind an extra week, to help our mom, a little longer. Then she'll have to fly back, north, where they are from. We could see them again next year.

I have to walk by the laundromat to get home, where our grandmother is doing some laundry, while watching you. For this whole week you didn't have to go to a babysitter, but I still had to go to school. I knew the way home. Our grandmother will later say it's a good thing she saw me, trying to cross that busy intersection, the one that leads straight to the base, all that traffic, all by myself, that she was there to come out and stop me, tell me to stay right there.

4
Coast

WE FIRST KNEW VERA with her moled-skin because of our dad, before he went away. They worked together on the base. She was the one who started to side with our mom against him, when he first started to slip away, to drink too much all of the time. He'd no longer just drink over at Vera's. He was often supposed to go with us to Vera's that night, so we'd have something to do, but then he'd be too drunk, already. Then he just wants to stay home. We'd go alone, while he drowned in the couch, down in the numb of his deadened sleep.

We'd go with our mom. She needed someone like Vera to talk to, so she put us in the powder blue car. He'd be passed out soon enough.

THERE WAS NOTHING for us to play with at Vera's, not really. She fixes our mom a drink. She gets some of the channels we don't get, so we can watch some TV. She councils our mom, helps her, with stories about her own first husband. She still loves him. Somehow he died. Vera will start to cry, and then our mom will say something that changes things for a while. Vera would teach us to play cards, so we could pass the time while they talk. While trying to build houses with the cards, teaching ourselves solitaire, we listen. The great thing about this game was you didn't need anyone to play it with you. She had another pack of cards in her house somewhere. She knows she does.

It was at her house that we first learn to swim. It was her first husband, Stanley, who left her with the built-in pool. Her daughter Tammy was already getting ready to move out, already eighteen. We were still so young, our mom had a while before that. We could run outside in the backyard around the plum trees, where we'd pick Vera's plums before they were even ripe. She didn't want us doing that. This is something else to forget about one day. You'll grow up, go on with your life. Forget how alike we both were back then.

There's a picture we were partial to even then, of the three of us. In the water, in Vera's pool, we are all on our backs floating. You and I are small, and Tammy so much bigger. She has one of us on either side of her, arms under us under the water, and, slowly as we learned to trust her, she'd lower her arms out from under us. If we didn't panic, we'd stay up. We would be able to do it one day without even those orange plastic floats of water wings we'd pull up over our small white arms, have to, anytime we wanted to go in the deep end or out towards the middle. Someone had to help us put them on. If you wet them inside first, they slide on easier, the plastic didn't sting so much, going up over your arm, to just below the shoulder. We had to be calm and relaxed, on our backs, or we'd sink quickly without them, in an instant. The trick to float was to learn to let the mind go, to only think calm thoughts.

5

Father Bob

HIS ROOM WAS RIGHT ACROSS the road from the church we went to before our mom wanted to stop going, before later in life she finds she wants one to go back to. We went to his room once, because it's possible our mom might be in love with this priest. You could never be sure. We won't quite know what is going on. All we know is that day we were going to have to say goodbye to Father Bob. He was leaving. He had to go to another parish. We'd been going to the church just for him.

After his last service, our mom asks us to wait outside for her, in the church graveyard, after following him across the road back towards where he lives in a room inside that garden. She was going to talk to him alone. She wanted to say goodbye in private. It was important to her to get to talk to him one last time. It would only take a minute.

When we saw inside it, everything seemed so small. His room was nothing but a tiny bed in the corner of a hardwood floor. She was crying again, like we hated to see her.

Father Bob tells us to go on, turning to us in his room, her children. She'd be fine, he said, she'd be right out. He was just going to have another word with her, to help her, help her be strong. She had to be strong for us.

We are cold while waiting outside in thin, matching windbreakers. We shuffle around the graves and wonder why she still hasn't come back yet, why it is taking so long. We aren't sure.

It's the old graveyard of the church, where the priests now live. Only the priests could be buried there. The weeds growing everywhere. We find the names and dates imprinted in the stones. It's like across the street from our house, the lot of grass that only got mowed occasionally, shaded with many trees, where our dad would park his car when we first moved here, under one that dropped apples. We thought he might come back for it one day.

We'd both be older soon. We can't wait to belong there in the church, but our communion was never going to happen. You had to take classes, before you are able to take your First Communion, we are told. We don't have the money for the school. There in that part of the South, all the Catholics are rich. But I still have the rosary I was supposed to use.

I'll stop wanting to even touch my two fingers to the yellow sponge there in the holy water, as soon as you walked in the door. Everyone touches it. I know it's just water. Touching it to the middle of my forehead, the middle of my chest, and then each shoulder, starting with the left, crossing over, I say it burns.

AFTER FATHER BOB LEAVES, we don't really want to go back to the church. For a while our mom tries to tell us we'll learn to love the new priest just the same, just as much, though she doesn't seem to believe it herself. We all say how handsome Father Bob was. She says she loved Father Bob, too. It's going to be hard for all of us.

We go for a couple more weeks to sit in the red velvet upholstered pews. If you were going to cry there you had to cry silently. You had to sit still. What we do reflects upon her. We don't want to embarrass her. They all already stare at us because we always sit in the back. She says we have to, because we aren't technically members. Our mom doesn't want them bothering us. And this way we can slip out quietly before the service is over, if we want, while everyone else was receiving communion. Then there was just the closing prayer.

The service starts with the mass music. The new Father enters. All rise. The Father is followed by boys in white robes like angels. The older the boys, the shinier, the closer they got to stand next to him and the gold cross carried. The boys carry crosses on sticks, gold plates, and white flowers for the altar, smelling sickly, sweet. The long robes of white and satin are trimmed in gold thread laces. Their faces are all flush, healthy. The body and blood of Christ is given to those who go up there. It doesn't really mean anything, communion, our mom tells us. It doesn't matter. As they all go past, proceeding up the aisle, I turn my head to stare at the panes of stained glass.

OUR MOM WASN'T GOING to church anymore, not even to sit in the back, but she doesn't want to keep us from going. We'd then start going to with whomever would take us. We should go if we want. It doesn't really matter what religion the church is, she'd say. If you go, that's all that matters. Or what you believed in your heart. On Sunday, she'd wake us up early, and we'd get up and get dressed so that Roman and Troy's grandmother could come by to pick us up for church. We'd go with them, Roman and Troy, who lived just next door. Their mother's name was Cathy. They live in apartment C of the red brick triplex, and we live in A.

Both of us like Troy the best. Mrs. Jones will be out in front of the house, beating the car horn. Our mom would now have some time alone in the house. We could join their church if we want, but Mrs. Jones tells us until we do we have to sit in the back. The rest of them all walk forward, Mrs. Jones, the quieter husband, Roman and Troy.

Every week at their church there's the moment in the service when you can come forward with a small group of the brave, who feel they need to ask for the help of everyone else there to pray for them. You can whisper to the preacher what you would like him to cure you of, so he can help make your life better, and he will ask God, speaking in a low voice to the rest of the congregation waiting there for you to spit it out.

They'll pray for me. They'll help me heal, going to help me get better.

But I will be sick again that night.

Our mom told me not to get my hopes all up, like I obviously was, so I won't want to go to church with Mrs. Jones and Roman and Troy anymore. She's never forced us to go. We don't have to go, our mom says. She says if I don't want to go not to worry about it.

There is the gentle but insistent shaking every morning from our mom's hands, on me right before she is about to leave for work. I have to take pills every morning, capsules that are easier to swallow, two, every morning in bed. She's wearing the clothes you have to wear to work in the hospital, her clean solid colors, a deep purple maroon, or a sterile, seasick green. These clothes for work are loose and baggy and swallow much of her. We are on our way out the door, to leave bright and early in the morning. Every day begins with the medicine before I am really awake. It's the only way I'll get in all I need every day. Sit up just enough to take the pills she cups in her hand. The stronger I get, once my allergies come less frequently, I can then go down to just one pill every morning, one just before supper. You can tell it is almost time for me to take my medicine by the way my breathing will change, but sometimes I can't take another of the pills yet. Sometimes I'll have to wait.

Before there are these pills twice a day, there is the portable breathing machine our mom brings home for me from the hospital. She's made special arrangements to be able to. This way she doesn't have to be always taking me up there, when I can't manage to catch my breath. Sometimes she says we might as well live there. Back at home, I suck on the plastic mouthpiece, connecting to the tube that hooks to the machine, inhale deeply, hold that mist of the medicine down in the lungs, then blow out. Again. I do this treatment at the kitchen table. We leave the machine there for me, pushed off to the side sometimes. It isn't all in my mind. I know I need it, but I never want to admit it when I do. She can see when there is something wrong with me, like you could, too, when you had to call her. It's not OKAY for me to go play outside, or I have to take a breathing treatment, as soon as I come back in.

When it happens in the middle of the night, I have to go wake her up, to tell her, to say I think I might need to take one of my treatments. So she then has to get up, when she had to get up for work in just a couple of hours, to set up the machine, put the medicine in it, at the kitchen table. I sit there for the forty minutes or so it takes, in the middle of the night, or the early morning, while you and other boys in other houses sleep. Sometimes I wake you up, too. Sometimes it helps to just breathe in the steam of a hot shower, which I believe I can do without waking anyone up. I think what I need to do is wet my lungs. I don't like to try to wake her up as much these days because she's more often not alone. He's in there with her, the new man who's going to become our dad before too long, our stepfather, the one who takes us all to the zoo one weekend before he's there always now. She really likes him. At the zoo when I get upset she tells me she's warning me. She's not playing with me. Why can't I just enjoy something for once?

Because he's not my dad. I'm embarrassing her in front of him. She's sorry about me.

There are headaches along with the allergies. I'll call softly outside her bedroom door. They are all part of it. The headaches go away sometimes, if I can just make myself throw up. The headaches can wake me up in the middle of the night, too. I'll lie there, trying to see if they are getting worse, if I am starting to feel any better now that I am awake.

SHE BRINGS ME a glass of water with my pills, but before long I grow used to them, and I've learned how to coat them, slick their outsides enough with whatever wetness there is already in my mouth, push them down my throat by just swallowing really hard. Some mornings I am still so tired, so far out in the middle of some dream I am having, her padding in takes longer than usual to rouse me. If I'm not awake enough though, if I fall back asleep before I've finished swallowing, the shell starts to melt, sticks to the roof of my mouth, gums, bitter, half-dissolved, cement-like shapes glue on my teeth when my mouth starts drying out again. When the alarm for school goes off, and I wake up a second time, my mouth will be full of this taste. I opened my eyes just a bit to the glint and shape of her uniform, the white she's wearing some days. She hands me my pills and kisses me goodbye. We should always do that, because you never know. Something could happen, and it could be the last time you saw each other.

6

Girl Scouts

WE ARE STILL YOUNG, so they think it won't really matter, our mom and our babysitters, Sue and Richard. Sue and Richard are in charge of a Girl Scouts troop, the Brownies. They'd only be able to watch us on the days they have Brownies if we can go along with them for the meetings they conduct. There's Richard, but he's a grownup, the husband of the Den Mother. I won't feel out of place there, I know already. I won't mind that there are no other boys in sight. Though I will at first be a curiosity for the girls, who find it odd that I am with them there. It's not long before they will see I am just like them.

The Brownie meetings take place on the base in a building made of mostly metal, a shelter house. Along with you, me and the other girls walk around duck ponds. The older girls, next door, they're not Brownies, they're Girl Scouts. There's a difference. They are old enough, and they notice what's wrong with me, I shouldn't be there. But I don't want them to say anything, the way I'll go up to Richard, while we learn to make cookies. It's a skill. I am waiting for the day someone's going to say something loud enough that Sue and Richard will change how they really feel about me being there. We're baking the cookies so that they can become ornaments for the Christmas tree. Another day we make jewelry with beads, iridescent, sparkling, that catch the light when you move them. We use red velvet and evergreen pipe-cleaners for more projects, gluing this and that, old newspapers and the paste we made ourselves to construct our model volcano. They usually only do that in Boy Scouts, Richard says, but all the young girls insisted, and since I was there. It was what they wanted to do more than anything. They begged. I still think of Sue and Richard as like brother and sister, although they are married. They are that set together. He comes with her to Brownies always. He says he'll come to make me feel more comfortable, though I don't really need him.

On those days when we don't have Brownies, we entertain ourselves at Sue and Richard's with what they keep in an old clothes basket, pink plastic or blue or yellow. It is filled with old toys, dolls left over from the girls they've babysat in the past, old credit cards no longer worth anything or blank ones, the extra checks for closed accounts, and all the old purses Sue doesn't want anymore. Then one day they have to tell our mom they are stationed somewhere else. That's part of life in the Air Force. They have to go. Our mom is disappointed, just as upset as us, she says, but she promises she'll find us a new babysitter we'll like just as much as we did them, who were going to have to stop taking us to Brownies, anyway. She was going to have to start finding someplace else to take us on those days. Some of the mothers of the older girls, with their troop next door, had started complaining, about how I had no business there, about how I shouldn't be around there with their daughters.

7

The Nursery

AT CINDERELLA, you and I would be separated into different rooms for a year because of our ages. We'd sleep on the cots at nap time after lunch. You get to go with the young black lady who makes the fish sticks on Fridays, into the room she oversees, because she watches the younger children and the babies. Our mom tried to see if there was any way they could not separate us.

It is hard to fall asleep with all the other strange bodies around you, the strange sounds they make. The darkness is made artificially, by blankets being hung up over the windows at noon. We thought the first women who ran the nursery, three sisters, loved us. We were their favorites, they told our mom, you with your blond pigtails, me with my bowl. But then there's the new owner, who would take over and change the name, to show it's a different place now, Cinderella has become Snow White. But we'll keep going to Snow White. There was nowhere else to go really, nowhere else new or better that she could afford. I would never know what to do with myself at recess at the nursery, either, like at school. If you were a boy, they won't like you to just stay on the swings. They'll get mad, tell you to do something else. Boys should be over there with all the others who are playing army dodgeball. In kick ball, when I'm up, why can't I ever manage to just land my foot where it should go? I just need to concentrate on it, coming my way. They had a huge sandbox, filled with babies, kids who couldn't really talk yet. It's under trees, so it's always cool and damp in there. We had a turtle in the backyard, in a cardboard box, but the man who was going to move in let it go. It was cruel to do that to an animal. It was not ours, even if we found it. If I pretend like I'm the dad, they say at the nursery, it's okay for me to play in the sandbox with the littler kids.

BEFORE SHE REMARRIED, our mom took us once to the drive-in with her. She was going with this man we didn't know. Our dad still hadn't come back yet. That night she knew we'd be asleep in the backseat of the sky blue car, that was hers, she was keeping it, in no time.

Sound comes from the speaker hooked up onto one of the car's windows, rolled halfway down. You can make it go all the way up, but then it's harder to hear. The sound was piped in to us. The movie was something scary is all I can remember. We might be scared, too, by being out there in the middle of nowhere with this man. He drives us far down the highway out to the place. It is dark, and like another world, to see all the cars just sitting there, all parked, going nowhere, all available attention asked to be directed up towards the same point in the sky. It's like at home when we watch one soap opera, all three of us together, as soon as our mom picks us up from the nursery and we get home, before he is there in the house with us then. We all are watching it, as a family, happen, as one of the characters tries to kill herself. We don't quite understand yet what it means, when she turns on the gas on the stove, at the end of the scene. What was happening, we asked, and our mom tried to explain it to us, the best she could, though we still wouldn't really understand why.

WE ALL SAT AROUND in a circle on the floor, the ring we made with our bodies so big it takes up the whole of the big playroom. Who you got to sit next to, who let you sit next to them, this meant something, just like it mattered who touched who on the head, if they made you duck or goose.

It mattered who chased who, who was in pursuit, who got who, like it mattered who was the farmer, his wife, cheese, the rat. Like it mattered who stood alone.

Mrs. Mary Alice has a son. He's always there at the nursery, helping his mom, folding after naptime blankets from the cots, while everyone else runs out in the yard. Even though he is still a kid, just a little bit older than us, it is like he works there. He's almost as awkward as they see me. It doesn't seem to matter to him how much younger than him you are. He likes you a lot. He is tall, especially for his age, and he carries you around like you are still a baby. He and his mom, they are very religious, and they are public about it, too, although she'd never try to push it on any of us at the nursery, she says. There is a time and a place for that. She promises our mom that.

I've decided I'm going to be her son's close friend, since most of the other kids at the nursery think he's weird. His skin is so white. He doesn't go outside much. He doesn't have to, because he's the owner's son. He'll help in the kitchen. I'm going to save him. I carry around little blue figurines with me, a bit like plastic army men, but they are different. They do better things. They are thicker. I like to have at least one with me always. I keep them in my pockets.

His name is Michael. Michael isn't allowed to have any toys, because he might without his even knowing it start worshiping them like false gods. I have all of my stuffed animals at home I've allowed to mean more to me than most living things. You can see it in the way I place them on my bed, especially the koala bear I've named after one I've seen in a book in the library. It is ridiculous to cry over them, and to keep any of them for too long. Come on, they're just stuffed animals. But you can imbue anything with anything. That's one of his mom's biggest fears. She is suspicious of my influence.

I bring the small blue men with me to the nursery, and I talk to you and our mom about Michael. I've been planning on giving him one. I don't bring any of the stuffed animals to the nursery with me. That side of myself I'm keeping at home. Michael acts young for his age, but you have to realize you're still too young for a boyfriend, so don't say you'll be his girlfriend. He can hide what I give him in his cubbyhole, where his mom won't see it.

His mom can't believe some of the things people spend money on. Mrs. Mary Alice says the devil has his eye on me. I might as well have a pacifier. My grandmother sends the men to me. His mom doesn't have to buy Michael any, because I'm going to give him one.

Mrs. Mary Alice doesn't want anyone thinking he is getting special treatment, just because he is her son, so he's got a place to store his stuff like all the other kids at the nursery, his name on a label for his own cubbyhole, where his jacket is. And I can put one of my men inside one of the pockets. He'd find it later.

His jacket is on top of the coloring books he has with only religious pictures in them, blank crosses that should be colored in yellow or brown. She screams at the top of her lungs his first and last name together. She grabs him, and starts shaking him back and forth, right there in the nursery in front of all of us. He's trying not to cry, and that's why Michael's face is getting all red.

He won't say anything, just let her shake him back and

forth, take it. She'd throw my present in the trash, but I'd fish it back out. And he should have known better. I've been putting ideas in his head, about what he needs. I'll be punished, too. When everyone else goes on that upcoming field trip, even Michael, I won't go, won't get to go see the horses. I'll have to stay there and play kick ball with the other kids whose parents won't sign the permission slips.

ONE GIRL WAS SENT to the nursery with a plastic bag full of sugar cubes, something we got sparingly at Snow White on special days like Fridays, and then only if they were all out of marshmallows, of which every kid would normally get to have only one. The sugar cubes in the bag in her cubbyhole melt in my mouth, one after another, before anyone could prove anything, and it was her word against mine.

YOU WERE PLAYING HOUSE. As for me, whenever, wherever the army dodgeball slams into me, I have to pretend like I've lost that part of my body. Right leg, so hop around on the left for the rest of the game. If you fall, that means you're out. The winner would be the last one left standing, no matter how many limbs they had missing.

They keep telling me I'm not really hurt, that I'm just trying to get out of playing with everyone else, again. Mrs. Mary Alice comes out into the backyard of Small World, we've followed her from Snow White, and tells me to quit my crying. But my arm is swelling. The girl who watches all the babies feels sorry for us, and she doesn't really like Mrs. Mary Alice. We can tell. And she believes me. She knows I'm really hurt. I keep clutching my purple arm, I won't stop crying, it feels like it's pinching all inside me. Our mom would be there in two more hours to pick us up. They were not going to call her just because I fell.

I do get to come inside, though, while you stay outside and play house. I have to sit at one of the cleared tables, where we eat our lunch earlier in the day, and put my head down on the table, if I feel like I need to come inside. Try to fall asleep, to make it stop hurting. I've felt it feeling this way before. It's broken. I know it's broken.

One of us is still playing outside when our mom finally gets there. She doesn't really think there's anything wrong with me, Mrs. Mary Alice. Our mom says she can tell just by looking at my arm that it's broken, how couldn't she?

She drives back to the hospital she just left, after they bring you inside. A doctor wraps over my arm first in bandages, then over that limb in plaster. For the fever, I should take aspirin and sleep. Once I go back to the nursery, that next day, I'll say see, cast on my arm, cradling it, the bone inside that will never heal quite right. There are more breaks the longer you live. Once I'm older, dancing wherever I go, I twist one ankle, repeatedly, keep coming down on it too hard. It gives out again later, after wearing a brace for a couple of weeks. I try to make it a joke, this thing about me.

He was a weakling, our mom says, saying one of the few things she says about our dad, after the fact of him. Also how he never hurt us kids, though we'd convince ourselves how he was ugly, given how badly he'd hurt our mom.

8

A Vet

WHEN WE ARE STILL in our first house, I am still light enough to climb far up that apple tree across the street, to stare down at the white car under. In that tree, if I climb higher, up to the very top, I could get higher than the roof of our house even. I could look down on that, too. You'll never follow me that high up the tree, though. Climbing even higher is one of the dares Roman and Troy and later others make I take up every time. One day I would jump out, believing my breast, my weight, eating habits really enough like that of a bird for me to land in my own good time. If I just believe, I will sail. But I come crashing down in a heap on my splintered bone, and you scream, as you are pulling up in the sky blue car, the Torino, with our mom. I was supposed to be staying in the front yard, and playing with Roman and Troy.

I want to show our mom how I was not afraid. I've climbed up to where the branches are the thinnest, limbs tapering out, the start of new leaves. I've waited for you and her to drive up, to get back from the store just up the street. As she's parked the car, opened the door, and walked around to your side to help you out, I call out. Look up. My head is protected by my land on my arm. It's the first of the three times I've broken that arm.

In the yard of Small World, I play something deep inside my head while I swing, something we watch on TV. It isn't a bad thing that the characters on the show all always wear the same clothes. That's how you know who they are. I go higher and higher in the swing, pretending like it's me driving the car. Sometimes in my head I'm being both the smart one and the one everyone sees as pretty. There's only one boy for the two of them. The car is swinging wildly out of control. Jerking side-to-side the chains, I tell myself watch out, we're going to have to jump. Not until after landing can I see what's gonna happen. I'm thrown forward, my ankles giving way underneath me, catching myself landing on the arm I've broken before, now again.

OUR MOM WILL REMIND us he's never hurt us, whenever we complain about the occasional, uncontrollable temper of the man she's met to live with us. When he calls the guinea pigs we keep in a cage rats, she doesn't understand why I'm getting so upset. After the guinea pigs, we had the hamster, which somehow gets out of the cage and that we never see again. It has to be somewhere in the house, or it doesn't make it any sense. I say it couldn't have just gotten out.

We expect now being asked what we want to be when we grow up. If you don't know yet, I do. I'm going to be a veterinarian. I rehearse my response. Our mom thinks I'm being unrealistic, it's more than about just loving something. There's more to the job than that. Do I really have any idea what all I'd have to do? An animal can't hold a thermometer in its mouth. They are like babies. You know how babies get theirs taken. Do you really want to do that, day in, day out, for the rest of your life? You'd have to help them have their babies, too.

She wants to try to be open with us, to talk to us kids. She never wanted us to feel like there was anything we couldn't talk to her about. I'm sleeping naked some nights, because she said it could be good for your skin, to let it breathe. We don't have any clean pajamas. We learn how to keep still, fall asleep, to trust the present isn't going anywhere, once you close your eyes. In the middle of the night, I start holding onto myself.

I dress weird. She hopes one day I will grow up to be more normal, more like other boys. She wants to protect us both. We have no names on the back of our jeans.

To teach us about sex, she takes us into her room, one at a time, each of us in private. She wants to know if we have any questions. We'll share our information. I've started believing everything the boys my age at school say they do. One Mexican boy in particular is always bragging. He'll come to school, talking about what all he's done over the weekend with girls. They all listen to him. In her room, I tell our mom if I really wanted to be like everyone else, I should start having sex. She doesn't believe they're really doing that. You just don't want us to grow up, I tell her. She won't even let us go out to the skating rink, on Friday or Saturday night, where everyone else goes. She says they're just lying. A boy my age couldn't even get hard if he wanted to. I ask her how she knows, he's Mexican.

I knew a bit what the talk was going to be about, from you. We are supposed to go into our room after the talk, and think about it. If we have any questions, we could come back, knock on her door. She'd be waiting inside there for us. We could trust her. I pretend like it is happening to me, that I know what that means, to get hard. See, he could be, if I am.

I want a way to be closer to him, that Mexican boy at school, so we could be friends. Though it's not like I could ever go out anywhere with him. If he does what he says he does, she's really not letting me go with him to the skating rink on the weekends. When she tries to explain, I start to think about Christy, who we take our clothes off with, when her dad watches us. I'm beginning to be afraid it may already be too late, that I may have already gotten her pregnant, with the way I'd rub up and down, along her, what we do. I still think that this is all you have to do.

9

Billy's House

CHRISTY WOULD SHOW US what was her favorite picture, this naked man in the encyclopedia. She goes and gets the book, and turns to the entry. His legs are crossed, crossed in such a way that they are pushing together at the inner thigh, raising up the man's privates, up into the air. I want Christy to like me like that, too, to see I'm like that. I'm just like that man in the picture, got what he's got. I could do that pose any time she wants.

She doesn't believe me. Christy closes the bedroom door, while I pull down my pants and try to arrange myself like the man in the book, looking at the picture, looking back at myself. While I get ready, you have to close your eyes. Then you could look.

You are a little embarrassed being there, but you want to see, too. You don't want to have to leave, to be shut out of the room. You've seen it before, you say. I'm your brother. You have something that Christy doesn't, a brother. We used to take baths together. Christy says that this is the way babies are made, taking off your pants and rubbing up and down there, rubbing the two different parts together. She wants me to do it to her, rub my body up against the whiteness of her pink there on the carpet. Some Saturdays we'd do it on the bed, but I like better to be on the floor. Some Saturdays we do this in front of cartoons, on the couch and under blankets, until it begins to hurt. Her dad Billy is babysitting us. I rub myself against her until it begins to sting. Then I have to stop. But sometimes she wants to do it more, again later. That's what we do over there. She is with her dad on the weekends, now that her mom wants a divorce. Christy gets a blanket from her bedroom, wants me to get under it with her. Billy is sleeping right then. If we are quiet, he could sleep all morning, going back to bed after our mom drops us off, over there early in the morning, on her way to work at the hospital. We'd have to be quiet.

To me, what I see is a tiny pink leaf, little up there inside between her legs. I'm curious but queasy. Like yours. We part our legs for each other. I imagine the feeling of a sponge, eventually all its pores filled. I look down to the side, off at the carpet, involve my eyes with being rooted there.

AFTER WE PLAY this game Christy calls poke-a-dot, I'll leave you and her alone in her bedroom, go off into the bathroom, because I like to be alone afterwards. Later in the day, she's going to want to play modeling again. The game can also start from that. We'll go into her bedroom and take off our clothes to walk around for each other. If I get a chance, I sneak off into Billy's bedroom, where he now sleeps alone. He's keeping the house. He reads books so big that I don't know how he does it, but I want to try to read one. We could talk about books, then. His are up against the wall by his bed, stacks of them, one or two he's in the middle of now on his nightstand. He reads every night before he goes to sleep. More books and magazines were strung along the floor, along with the clothes he's been in. Jeans are turned inside-out. There are lots of things to touch in there. Nobody picks up after him anymore.

When somebody else was in the bathroom in the hall, that was another excuse to go in Billy's room. There's another bathroom connected to his bedroom. Sometimes I say I thought someone was in the one in the hall, that's why I was going in Billy's room. He catches me sometimes in there in the dark, where it smells like rest, his sheets, all the shades pulled down to keep it cool during the day.

WE GO OUTSIDE to jump on the trampoline, and there Christy starts to boss us around. It's her house. After a couple of weekends, she begins making deals with us, so we'd keep doing it. We'll take turns with you, so you don't feel left out. She says she's gonna tell, if we don't. She'll say it was my idea, I made her do it. He'll believe her. I don't want Billy mad, so again in the corner of the room with the stone blue flat carpet that burns your elbows and knees, I do this with Christy, while I think I know what it must feel like for Billy to live all alone. Our mom still hadn't found anyone else yet, that's why he was watching us. He's so nice, I tell her, liking to talk about him to her. I'm worried about him, I say.

He'd see us again next weekend, but I didn't want to go, not yet. I wasn't ready to go back to our house. I want her to stay there with Billy, with us. Just one more hour to play. Doesn't she think he is handsome? She says she's sure he'll get married again, soon. It's hard for her to be impartial, because even though he watches us on the weekends and Billy is a nice man, the woman he's divorcing works with her, and she's still her good friend, she says.

WE SPEND PART OF one Christmas over there at his house. We'll take some presents over, save some to open over there. The three of us kids pose for a picture under his barely decorated tree, with a few strands of silver tinsel, not spread out right. To our mom he has said something about me, something I didn't hear completely, not all of, something about the way I've started to act more. I've heard him say something like this on another day, to one of the guys who comes over to drink at his house. He was supposed to be watching us. Look at me. Look at how I walk around. Our mom was working a double that day, because she needed the money. She still hadn't come to pick us up, yet. We were tired of being over there then for so long, but we might have to sleep there that night. Someone just doesn't show up for work. She couldn't turn down the money. If they asked her to stay, she has to, she says. She wants to keep her job. I was going to tell her as soon as I saw her how I didn't want to go over to Billy's anymore, how I didn't think he was a good babysitter.

10
Jessup

WE'D NEVER KNOW too much about all the other ones, girlfriends from before, who loved this new man before our mom would. She was going to be the one to marry this friend Billy had, and the women from before, they were eventually going to lose track of him through her. A couple of them will have the nerve to call our house, trying to track him down, just to see how he's doing, they say, but they were not going to be getting him back now. They say they were just curious to see what he's been up to these days. There's something our mom has that makes her special.

They met at a party at Billy's house. Our mom was still trying to be strong, but she needed to have some fun every now and then, too. Billy's wife at the time and the other women at work have been telling our mom she needs to let go more. The night of the party, she has us get into our pajamas, before loading us into the car, then driving over to Billy's. We could go to sleep tonight over there, in one of the back bedrooms, Billy's room or Christy's, away from all the noise, his wife offers. Our mom just wants to enjoy herself a little bit. She'll be right out there in the living room, she says. If we need her, all we have to do is call her. She'd take us back home later. She might not stay that long, just a couple of hours.

Christy is already in bed, sleeping. Our mom tries not to wake her up, bringing us in, but Christy's disoriented. It's hours before any of the adults will be going to bed.

We can't blame her for wanting to have some fun. She's working hard to keep us fed, and she doesn't know what to do with us. He's this man she's met at this party, and he's going on a trip soon to the woods. Some weekends that's what he does. He's going to hunt deer. He wants our mom to come. He's asked her if she wants to join him, up in the woods. There would be some other men there, too, his friends. Don't worry. We won't be all alone.

She can't find a sitter for us, can't really afford one, but she won't want to tell him that. Still, she wants to be with him. She wants to go. He tells our mom she doesn't have to worry about finding a babysitter. She can just bring us along, her kids. There would be things for us to do. Anyway, we've been begging her to let us go, because we don't want her to leave us, not for a whole weekend. So we promise we'll stay out of her hair. The other men he's going hunting with are leaving on Friday, once they all got off of work for the weekend. They wanted to get out of town as soon as they could.

They'd be hunting for food for their mothers, their girlfriends, and their few wives. Back at the houses, they all have big deep freezers that they fill up with the packages wrapped in white paper, with red marker dates scribbled on the outside. Cuts of deer meat, our mom says, when he gives us some for ourselves. She tells us it tastes just like any other meat. If they get one deer, that's enough to eat for all winter. It's good, she tells us. You can cook it in soups, and we'd never know the difference. There's no reason to cry about eating a deer.

The place where they are going hunting is called Jessup. It is cold there, where they are going. He tells our mom, to make sure we know. We better bundle up. There won't be any heat in the small cabin in the woods where we'll all be staying. We're gonna be the only children there. Will there be any food besides deer meat? How far away is it? How far into the woods, how far away from home?

She won't know what to do with us, once we get there. She says it's called roughing it. There's no phone there.

The men we are with, they all want to enter the woods as completely as possible, for as long as they are able to stand it. In the cabin, which is never used for real life, there's some candy in the jar in the corner, up high on a wooden dresser. One of the men will take it down for me, once our mom says how I won't stop asking about it, when they get back from hunting for the day. They might go back out that night. I can go ahead and eat some of the candy if I want, eat all of it, but who knows how long it's

been sitting there, who even brought it. It's probably been
here forever, the one whose parents own the land in the
woods tells us. I want it, because I'm hungry. But in my
mouth it won't have any taste. It's like a bunch of dust. It
comes apart in an instant in my mouth. I try to pretend
like it's good, but they don't believe me, when they ask me
what it tastes like.

She says we're going to be fine here, with the bare
refrigerator that hardly works. I open and close it, but the
light inside doesn't come on when you open it. We go out
for a walk, with our mom, through thickets, briars, under
branches. Watch your legs.

Early the next morning, the men are all off hunting.
Time is out of order, because we got there so late last night.
A fire was already started, by some of them who had come
up hours earlier than us, got there in the early evening. The
puddles we walk past in the woods are all frozen. I hold
onto one of our mom's hands, you take the other. Though
older, I'm still stumbling every couple of steps trying to
keep up. Your cheeks are bright blood red. We'll go back
inside to the fire soon. Our mom wants to get rid of some
of the boredom of just sitting there in the cabin.

During the night, she shares a sleeping bag with him.
We go together into a separate room. The rest of the men
sleep in front of the fire dying down, listening in case any
deer come up close to the cabin.

They carry thermoses strapped over their arms. All of

them are good friends, real close, they all work together. They are trying not to mind too much the presence, the intrusion, of our mom and us. We're gonna go back home in a couple of days, but we wanna go before that.

Go color, she says, when we tell her we're bored. I flip through the pages of a book, color. Quit your whining. We're not going home yet. You shouldn't have come. We're the ones who wanted to come so bad. She says she warned us it was going to be like this, that the woods weren't really a place for children. You could go take a nap. She'd wake us up before supper.

I'll play with your dolls, since they are the only toys that have been brought along, on this special occasion. I can play with them, but I have to promise to be extra quiet. Go into the other room, she tells us, so when they come back we won't be in their way. I want you to help me figure out a reason why there might be two moms in one family, because I don't want to be the dad.

The windows were not real windows. That's one of the reasons why it's so cold up at the cabin in Jessup. Wherever the glass should be, there were sheets of plastic instead. That was layered with dust and dirt from the winter, and you could barely see out of it, into the air. I press my face against the flexible barrier, only shielding us partly. You could make out the trees, freezing, their needles, strands of icicles hanging off of them. We get to sleep on the couch the next night, in front of the fireplace with the men, if we promise to be good, not to disturb anyone, go straight to sleep. He and our mom were going to take the big bedroom, the one with the big bed. It would be warm there in front of the fire.

But someone would need to put more logs on it soon. They watch me moving around their feet, but they don't say anything. Then they tell me not to get too close, when I say I'm just watching the fire.

They drink, they fight, and they disappear. Our dad broke everything, all her plants that last night he was there, raving, before he took off, with all his anger and confusion. We watched him pick up one flower pot after another. She'd water them every day, in the morning or at night before bed if she'd forgotten earlier. He threw them against those white walls in the red brick house. When we then broke one of her plants, accidentally, we'd run to the end of the street, the end of the cul-de-sac, not wanting her to see what we'd done. We wanted to avoid any confrontation at all costs, because it would be our fault. At the end of the street, we hid, behind one of the houses we never saw anyone coming out of, and then heard her calling for us, to please come back, because she was scared she'd lost us.

One day, it's over. He's gone, and she's there to take care of us. Our real dad was just something we could no longer grasp, no longer remember all the details of, like we'd begin to forget how he looked even, moved through the house, affecting everything by every little thing he did.

11
Florida

WE WERE GOING to be taken off to Florida, to the beach, with our grandparents. This would give our mom a much needed break from the two of us. Nobody gets everything they want, like I've been wanting this one toy, waiting for one that lights up, a caterpillar that glows orange and bright, like the sun at night, or a night light you could hold in your hand and control yourself. These things cost money. But I'm directing all my thoughts here.

Off at the beach with our grandparents, I could have all the shells I want. Take them. Our grandmother says just make sure I get some good ones. Those ones she calls clamshells, cupping up flatly against the sand, are scattered, found, washed up everywhere. We don't want those. There are plenty of those. I try to fill white plastic bag after white plastic bag with the best I can find. I start over, try to get only the ones with unusual colors. I think I'll bring them home and line the porch with them. Hide some in the yard. I'll ruin others by painting them with fingernail polish our mom keeps cold in the refrigerator, garish hues of red, brown, chocolate, tan, and purple she doesn't really use. You couldn't wear such colors at the hospital, because it won't look professional. Kept in the refrigerator door, the colors will last longer, won't start to clump. She lets me paint my toenails once, but only my toenails. It doesn't matter. Nobody at school will ever see because of my shoes.

Our grandparents park their mobile home in the lot where they can hook the traveling house up to water and electricity. We are told not to cry, when we start to get upset. A board game will take our minds off of things, late at night. Our grandmother promises us our mom will still be there once we get back, and if we are good, quiet, they might get me that toy.

Every time our grandparents pass through on their way down from Ohio, to Florida where they vacation for the winter, they bring us something. Our grandfather brings me the Emerald City, this cardboard box covered in plastic and painted green to look like it's from the movie. Slowly, one by one, he buys us the figures to go inside.

They teach us at the kitchen table Crazy Eights, Hearts, Spoons. Sometimes our mom would join us, but it's hard to play with an uneven number. We each got one of our grandparents to be on our team. One gets the girl, and one gets the boy, then we'll switch.

In Florida, our grandmother tells me follow her outside, quiet, quick, out to where the mobile home is parked.

Come here. My eyes are red and ready for bed, after the day at the beach, but I keep rubbing them, tasting the dark in the sea air. I stand behind her, then beside her, as she reaches her hand, a hand with lots of rings, bracelets on her wrist that go up and down her tanned arm, out over the fence which we've parked beside for the night. She's reaching over into the yard where someone really lives, year round, managing to get at one of the trees they have growing over there, one of its branches, pull it down and take four oranges bigger than oranges, grapefruits. One for everyone. I have to promise not to tell anyone, and it will be our secret. In the morning, everyone will wonder where they came from, they'll taste so good.

12

The Sea

ONCE, THE MAN who moves in took us to the sea, once before, the lake. There I'd build sand castles with seashells, up from a shoreline that kept creeping up. I kept swallowing mouthfuls of the sea, and you could tell we were really there. You could taste the salt. I laugh like a little girl. He tells me to calm down, or to stop screaming, when I run, yelling, squealing in that high-pitched voice too much.

We change into our swimming trunks together on the men's side. He has his darkness there, too, like our dad. Back home, he'll show us how to hide in the morning our pajamas under our pillows, that's a good place to keep them until the night. He learned that in the military. It's one of the things we do every morning now.

When I could still look him in the face, the new man in our house, meet his eyes, they are brown. One day they're going to make it official. He was not always going to be gentle with us. He hadn't much practice with holding onto children. You tend to become different when touched. His eyes were the color of fur.

He'd take us to the river. We go to the sea with him just that once. Our stepfather is there to raise us in the wake of a mirage. He takes us out in the boat on the water to catch fish. There are a number of lures we can use. Many things would work as bait. Crickets or grasshoppers, or worms packed down in containers filled with dirt, dark chips of damp wood. The blind red worms start their snaking about, through his fingers as they dig down into their environment, once opened, and they spin and slip, flipping over each other. He's looking for a good one, get a good one, removes it from where it's now been contained, to feel the air on its skin.

There are minnows, too, fish to catch fish with. They seem tame, with their slight silver bodies, silver tails you slip a gold hook through, piercing them down at their ends, towards the tails, there where they have no nerves. If you went too high up, they'd start to bleed. You wanted them still alive, when they went down into the water. They go back and forth in the air there, trying to swim. They go in clear circles, in the white, styrofoam coolers. The ice is kept in coolers like these, too. They're disposable, but you can reuse them, and we always do. A blue or red string is attached, just under the tight-fitting lid, to help you carry. They don't talk like the crickets and grasshoppers chirp. He shows us how snakes can swim. If you ever saw one, you'd only see the little black head, tongue forking out of a mouth slit open, above the lake glass top. They can make it all the way across. Water moccasins were the ones to watch out for.

He ties a rope around a tree branch, hanging out high from the shore over the lake. He pulls back the rope and hands it over to me. To swing out over the water. There were some places, if you jumped off of the boat, where no one had ever touched the bottom. You could kick your legs in vain, swimming down, no land anywhere in sight for miles and miles around. As far as you could see, there was just water, on every side, as you turned your body around in the water. There was a bottom, there had to be, although nobody could touch it. You could tell, because the boat's anchor had to be resting on something. We swam out in the middle where there was no chance of touching, but where when the anchor was pulled up later, the sludge, mud still covers it. Sometimes it comes up caked all red.

We joined hands in the water to have something to hold onto, kicking our feet even though we didn't have to, we had on life vests that would keep up. We rock up and down, back and forth in the waves, as other boats go by. The sun reflects off the water, up into your face. For the water and sun, we squint. Sometimes we wanted to see how deep down we could possibly go, if we could hold ourselves under even with the life vests on, even just for a few minutes.

We floated over in our life vests to the rope connected to the anchor, connected to the boat floating, rooted to this spot, picked out in the middle of the lake. We tried to pull ourselves under the water, under the surface, using the rope, scaling it backwards, fighting down against the water over our heads, and buoyancy that tried to pull us back up. Our hands downwards, trying to get as far down under the water as we could go, trying to touch the anchor, pushing our bodies under for as long as we could manage to hold our breath, open our eyes, though we won't see a thing, the water is too dirty, orange, turning our eyes red. Down there, it's swallowing us.

Back up, bursting, gasping for the air to refill our lungs. We wanted to figure out a way to breathe underwater. We couldn't reverse the process, though, blow out down there. We kept trying. We passed by in the boat cliffs of rocks where he tells us some people went to commit suicide.

There were certain things he feels I should be able to do. Sleeping by myself is one of them. Pretty soon I was going to have to learn how to sleep without a night light. Be a good sport. We're moving to a better block. My bedroom will be close to the one they'll share, and we'd each get our own bedroom, not like in the red brick house. We'll get a bigger yard, a bigger backyard. It was going to be better. In my new room, I'll never hear the trains outside again. They're not for people. I won't be woken in the middle of the night again. The tree outside my window will only the glass if it's windy. I rearrange and rearrange everything in my room.

I don't want anyone commenting on how well I throw, or the way I run. When he tackles me, I have to look up into his face, over on top of me. He's not wearing a shirt because it's summer, and it's hot. We can't help but be close when he's wrestling me. His chest is like a bear. He's going to teach me to fight for real, with what they call at school horseplay.

ALREADY IN THE WATER, I hold onto the rope that's tied to the anchor, sunk to the bottom, where he dropped it off. We've gone somewhere different for a change, the swamp he knows about. It's not good for fishing, but it could be a nice boat ride. It will be fun, our mom says. Nobody swam in the water out there, he tells us. They're scared of it. But you could. It wouldn't hurt you. It's so hot in the sun, I'm going in. The alligator rears its head up, going towards where it heard the splash, while I am swimming towards the sandbar, close, a tiny island like, not too far from where he's anchored the boat, for the best sun, the boat that rocks in the waves made when I jump off.

I don't see the alligator until I've started walking up the sandbar. Our mom shouts for me not to move. They can't move that fast, but they're bringing the boat. Stand still. It won't mess with me once they get me in the boat. Don't cry, remembering to camouflage.

13

The Holiday Inn

BEFORE HE GETS THE JOB fixing cars, our stepfather is a janitor for a little while. In addition to the five days a week, our mom was still working almost every weekend, and we were still too young to be left alone. On the weekends that he had to work also, pull an extra shift, he'd take us to the hotel where he cleaned rooms mornings after they were left. He only has to be there until he gets through all of the rooms that had to cleaned for the day. Then he'd take us back home.

He leaves us alone after hustling us out of the old blue truck with heavy doors, up to one of the empty rooms, one they've put nobody in yet. We can stay there while he works. We have to be quiet. He usually looks for a room not on the ground floor, but up a flight of the outside stairs, up to the second story of the hotel. We'd be better off up there. These mornings of winter have a blue air and light. He turns on the TV in a room, cartoons for us, before going off to make his rounds, and we watch while lying down across one of the green bedspreads. He'd come by once an hour to check on us, just to see how we were doing. We're okay. Sometimes we've fallen back asleep on the bed in the dark of the room. Keep the curtains closed. Don't open the door to anyone. He'll use a special knock, to let us know it's him. He goes around to all the empty rooms and collects the laundry, the damp towels, used linens. He brings home to our house every so often a box of the bars of small guest soaps, wrappers printed with the hotel's logo, green on white. This way our mom wouldn't have to buy any for a couple of weeks. He'd also bring home some of the white, thin towels marked across, in raised letters, their lengths, stitching spelling out the name of the hotel. He stole them, I tell our mom, one day when I'm trying to say why I don't like him. It didn't matter. They weren't important. They were just towels. Where did I think we got the other new set, ones with the word Hospital blue in the middle of the white.

FIVE DAYS A WEEK he would then dress in a gray shirt that will better hide the grease that will drip down off of axles, under cars suspended above ground, on supports made so he'd be able to easily slide underneath and adjust things. He'd make them as good as new. His leg muscles hid in dark gray pants collecting stains from bending down all day, in the general clutter of the garage. He has to remove his work boots before he enters the house, because of the grease, along the tops of the steel reinforced toes, on the bottom of the rubber traction soles. He wipes his boots on the doormat, and his rub back and forth, hard, repeatedly, will print there, every night under the force of all his weight. It doesn't matter how much he wipes them. He still has to take them off. He sits down to unlace and remove them every night before he comes in. Our mom doesn't want grease tracked all through, staining the carpet. Furniture is another matter. There isn't time for him to undress every day, when he comes home for his lunch hour. There's only a limited amount of time. He puts a towel down wherever he's going to sit on the couch, eating his lunch in the living room, in front of the TV. They both wore uniforms.

IT WASN'T LONG before our mom wanted to talk to us about the possibility of not going to the nursery anymore. It would help save money. We were old enough to stay at home by ourselves. She writes all the numbers down by the phone, assuring us somebody would always be there if we called, don't worry, somebody has to be at the hospital. Did we think we could handle it?

During the day, we'd pretend the bathtub was a hot tub, our jacuzzi. On other days, it was a swimming pool. We put our bathing suits on, sit on the side, getting the water as hot as we can stand, even if it's a pool today, it's a heated one, filling it up as high as we can, dangling our feet in together. If we ever needed her, all we had to do was call

73

the hospital and ask for her extension, which is easy to memorize. If she's not in the office, the switchboard can always page her.

During the school year, it's only an hour after we get out of school that we'd have to be alone in the house before she got home from work. We were to come straight home, walking home from school together now. As soon as we got in, lock and chain the door behind us. Summers were worse. Once she got home from work, we could go outside, but we couldn't leave the house during the day. She wanted us safe.

MY HAIR AROUND THIS TIME is still so blonde it's almost white in the sun. One would never mistake me for his. I am certainly not his son. He was so much darker than us. I watch him out in the yard in the garden he's making. He is going bald already.

Our mom tells us about the time she asked him about the war he was in, when she wanted him to tell her what happened to him there, but he doesn't want to talk about it. He won't for a long time. He's not ready yet. He had fired guns every day, just for practice, to make sure they would be ready.

We don't have one, but dogs bark up and down the street, jump their fences, come over into our yard, knocking over the garbage can and ripping into the bags, pulling the trash out across the yard. This neighborhood is getting worse, he says, going to Hell. I know, simply from our mom. She goes to lay down after work, before she starts supper. All the apartments one block over were being turned into government housing. We drive through the new projects, more, every morning, when he takes us to school. He wants to get out of that neighborhood. There's always shit in the streets, in all the front yards. Look at this. These people just throw their trash into the streets, our yard, anyone's yard. You'd better get out while you still can. Strays drag the trash from one to another. He says he's gonna shoot one of them one day, if he catches one in the yard one more time. If they belong to anyone, they better watch out. He's fighting a losing battle. I'm wearing the gold jacket my godmother sent me from where she works up north, Century 21. They sell houses. It's a real estate company, I tell everyone at school. She's the one I want to grow up to be like now.

14

The Life Force

WHEN IT'S THE SPORT he's taken up because he can't get away to go hunting so much, and when our mom is able to save up and get him new ones, we'll play with his old golf clubs. The owners of the garage where he works next after the Holiday Inn have gotten him a pass to a course. I rear back with one of the old ones, one day out in the yard, not noticing that you are still there behind me, and the dull thud is the iron silver rod against your forehead, slamming, splitting it wide open, so you run screaming into the house. I can't stop myself from crying, because you are so badly hurt. Our mom will have to keep telling me how you're gonna be fine. They're only rushing you off to the hospital for stitches, but you're gonna have another scar, like the one on your finger I gave you when we were younger and I'd go around the yard on an old broom, playing like I was flying off, riding. You'd want to get on with me. I go too fast and you slide off, trying to hold on, still, hands flying down the length of the old breaking wood, to catch, rip up against the metal edge of a barely still hanging hook for the broom, cutting open your finger. These times you are taken to the hospital before anything more serious happens, and there's what you'll have to get rid of, when you cry to them and beg for their help.

WE'VE STARTED CALLING him our stepfather, to the kids at school who ask, even though he hasn't actually adopted us yet. We use his real name to his face. This year we'll cut down a live Christmas tree, out at the tree farm. There they grow them just for this. We bring the saw with us in his truck, the one before he gets the new, nicer, if smaller, truck. It's hard always to open the old, heavy doors. You had to push hard to get out, pull hard, once you get in. Hunting and fishing, I should be doing that with him, not going shopping with you and our mom, whenever we just want to get out of the house, when we'd only look. We weren't going to buy anything. There's always that provision.

Out in more woods, he takes me behind the cabin his parents have there, a small trailer on some land out in the middle of nowhere, to show me where they kept the wooden plank set up especially for what we were going to do that day. We won't say anything on the way, while our shoes crunch against the gravel, poured out there to keep the area dug out for a driveway not so muddy when it rains. This path leads up there. He is going to teach me how to clean fish, under the old faucet outdoors. He lays out the catch, catfish and bass, but mostly just catfish with their bodies slick and like gray rubber on the sides and top, bellies white, then long whiskers and black eyes. One day knowing this might come in handy, he says. He takes out a big pocket knife, the one he always carries down deep inside the front pocket of his work pants. This weekend he's moved it to his jeans. The handle is brown, like his hair and eyes, his skin the color of late summer. Our hair is still being bleached by the sunlight to almost white. The knife is hard to open, with its heavy spring, and he wants me to try and practice opening it, tries to show me how to make the spring inside give without hurting you, release right. It can accidentally flip back on you, so be careful when handling it. Open the knife out away from you. Then he takes over. It's easy to slice through the skin of the fish with it. First you take off the head, saw through there. Then you flip the body, to make a slice that runs from one end to the other, all the way up to around the tail, opening the stomach. Cut off the tail. I should take the knife from him and practice, do it, run it under the cold water pouring from the faucet, to get it good and clean. Clean it all off. Once the body is open like this, you can scrape the guts out. Here's how you take out all of the bones, the skeletal structure that once held the skin tight and made it a way to float. That's what the inside of a catfish looks like. The tip of the knife point can be used as a wedge, like this, to take out the eye, if you want, in the future, but the head is going to be cut off anyway. Sometimes it's better than having them stare at you while you begin. Whatever you want.

Come here, he wants to show me something. Look at those globs of white. You see that? All up and down there, inside the mess of the pouch, in the body, those are its eggs. This one was pregnant. Those would have been babies one day.

ALL DAY LONG, long into the evening, first thing in the morning, there were loud guns. He was trained by their commands. The whistles they blew would before long fall on deafer ears. He'd had a lot of friends then, was close to a lot of men. They kept a lot bottled in. They got used to it. But it would all get released one day.

Hunting was one of the ways he used to unwind, but now that he was a little older, he went out to the woods with them all less and less. We could never really know what all he'd gone through, back then. Kids couldn't understand. Our mom tells us not to make fun of him for being hard of hearing. That's something he's sensitive about. He must tell all of the story to her, one night when they are alone, their door is closed, their voices hushed. They were constantly going off near him. She'd wanted to cry for him, she said.

He keeps the hunting rifle hidden under their bed. He

says he makes sure the safety is always on, anytime anything was said about this gun being in the house. In the living room, on some nights, he'd clean the long barrel with his towel oiled for it, warning us about it. A glass cabinet over at his parents' house is full of even more.

A gun was what he wanted to give me for Christmas. I like the color of the BBs. It was his idea. Our mom says she didn't even know he was getting it for me. He came home with it, already wrapped up, one day. When the floor of my bedroom is covered with the soldered drops, they'll then have something else to yell about.

For another Christmas, he buys me a football. I like that it is so new, how its clean shape feels in my hands, even knobbiness, rubber. I don't want to take it outside, put it on the shelf in my room. One night I take it down and play with holding it instead of a stuffed animal. This was someone's entire world.

Why don't I take the BB gun they got me for Christmas outside and practice shooting it in the backyard. You can shoot at beer cans, with colors of American flags stretched out over backgrounds of silver. Put a can up at one end of the yard, prop it up against the fence, aim for that, not the birds or squirrels. The life force was something to be respected. A gun was not a toy.

A little of the wet still left in the can, a few last drops, gets on my hand, going pink in the cold outside. I rub what I see as yellow in my mind against the leg of my jeans, turn another old can upside down, against the fence, old posts, back up towards the house, gun in my hand, do my best to line it up in the sight, cock, get ready again, aim. Imagine no one's watching me.

THERE WAS NOTHING he hated more than to be on his way home from work and to pass by one of the boys, black, who would come by looking for you, who would sometimes take me also on the handlebars of their nice bikes, for a ride, leaving our yard. On their bikes, your feet never had to dangle. Trick-pegs forked out from the front wheels and were a good place to rest your legs. They show us. Try to jump off just in time, to land in our yard, run in for supper, where we sit at the table silently, swinging feet under the table. He's telling us one last time how he doesn't want to see any of them in our yard again. He's already told us once.

HE TRIED TO TEACH ME how to drive the fishing boat, how to steer it over the glass top of the lake, safely, to avoid other boats. You steer this boat with the engine itself, the kind he has bought off of someone who was getting a new one, not one of the ones with a steering wheel. That's further up, but we sit at the back, with the handle attached to the motor, the blades, the end of it, submerged, chopping through the water to determine what direction we will take. Now I'm to take it, take control. Those boats are for pleasure. The kind we have is fine for fishing. He gets so tan in the sun because he's part Indian. They have Cherokee blood. Georgia clay won't come off your clothes. It stains everything, will cake on the bottom of your shoes, until you have to get them wet, scooping off the clay clumps in handfuls you'd flick to the side or rub into the tall green grass, or then it's all over your hands, fingers, palms, staining orange, red.

We lurched over a wave that made the boat bump up then slap back down, rocking everyone, throwing me into his hulk back there, his body without a shirt on, his chest a mat of curly black hair, tangled and deep, tight, the texture like that of moss on the rocks wet with rain or spray, waves, wet with the exertion of helping me steer over the lake, out in all that sun. There are drinks in the cooler, under a bag or two of ice cold. I drink an Orange Crush and sing a song on the radio.

My hands go with his, his on top of mine, to guide, help me steer some more. That's it. I was doing it. Then he'd try to slowly remove his. Now it was going to be all up to me. I'm driving the boat. The shell of its fiberglass rumbles, halfway in the air, before being submerged down into the next wave, like rocks rolling, the sound akin to something like pebbles crunching under his truck tires, ears tuned to a constant, steady, compacting beating down, muffling everything like cotton in and out of your ears or under sheets. It's hard for me to keep it pointed towards the center of the lake. He comes back, placing his hand back over mine, on top again, his completely covering over mine. You know it's all still there, underneath, as he takes the boat back from me, wrestling it back into some control, mine beating under there like it's been caught. He's sweating back at the helm of his boat, taking over.

15

He Moves In

AT FIRST, THERE WAS SO MUCH excitement. It just made sense. He'd move in before they got married, because it would help us save money. This was going to change things for us. He'd be better than our real dad. They'll make it official in a year or so, after they are more sure, once we are in the new house the extra paycheck helps us afford.

We think we will like living here, where my godmother and other relatives fly down to. Your godmother was on our dad's side, those people we'd never hear from again, mostly a shadow, like I would be for your own kids someday. They were going to have the wedding in our house. Someone's been hired to come over to perform the service. There'll be a cake. I'll wear a nice outfit, the nicest thing I have. Our mom will help us look through our closets. She doesn't want us playing in them, hiding from the rest of the house. She gets nervous when she can't find us. I try to see myself as just as pretty, in my own way, as I see our mom and you. We'd pretend other things as children. We play one game where something has happened to our mom, and we have to go and live with someone else.

I comb my hair over to the side, part it like it must have been our real dad showed me. Mark, make a line with the comb, wet my hair and take the two sides away from each other. It must have been him who took me for my first real haircut, if it wasn't our stepfather. Someone was taking me to a barber. You weren't going. Our mom wasn't going to have to keep trimming my hair at home. He wants it short, like his, up over the ears. As soon as I'm sat up in the chair, and he walks away from me, I start my bawling. The barber will just have to start cutting. He promised he wouldn't let it get too short. I'd grow out of it, these reluctances of mine. We pose for a family picture, me, you, our mom and him. The man who was going to be our new dad doesn't like it when I stand in front of the mirror too long, so hurry up.

When our mom leaves us there alone in the house with him, it will get quieter. We'll talk less. But he'll often ask if I've always been so skinny.

WHEN WE'RE DONE EATING, we're supposed to wipe off our placemats with the dishrag, then dry them with the towel hanging on the refrigerator door, after we put our plates in the sink. We should always clean them, he says, eat all of the cube steak she's cooked for us. She cuts it up into manageable squares for us at first, but then he thinks

86

we should know how to use a knife for ourselves. I hate the way the cube steak tastes, the tough tendons of gristle in my mouth, the parts they tell us to chew around and just swallow. It's not real steak. I get so bored, just sitting there. I was going to be the last one left at the table again that night, long after he'd already gone off to read the paper in the living room. Our mom has already started soaking the skillet she fried the food in. She's left it to sit, goes off into another room to get the clothes finished drying in the used machine he helped us get, had to fix, balancing it, replacing something, one little part, because that's all it needed to make these things as good as new. She'd save time and money, not having to go to the laundromat anymore. I pick up my fork, the silver prongs sharp enough to carve into the slick over the plastic orange of the placemats, scratching into mine, starting to draw designs. There's another color that hides underneath. I have to flip it over to try to hide what I've done.

From his mom, they've gotten an early wedding present, new glasses, something they could use. They're all so happy for him. His sisters joked about how they thought he was the last one of their brothers who would ever get married. He's never kept a woman for this long before.

Out in the yard, boys from other families are pretending they can fly, but on TV mine can only run really fast, and then she turns around and around to change herself, the only girl around them, the only girl on the glasses they all come on. You get one free if you buy enough to eat at one of the fast food places. Her glass was the one none of them wanted, and so Cathy said I could use it, anytime she watched us over at her house with Roman and Troy, until the day it's broken in their dishwasher, but there's no reason for me to be crying the way I am.

The boys from other families in the neighborhood are playing cops and robbers, cowboys and Indians, when they're not playing superheroes, wearing their special underwear outfits made especially for such boys, matching tops and bottoms underneath their clothes, hiding for now secret identities.

OUR MOM SAYS she isn't wearing white to the wedding because it isn't her first time. White is only worn that first time. That too is why they aren't having the wedding in a church. One of the reasons. She's wearing brown, won't even a dress, a brown skirt and blazer, also brown, a cream-colored blouse. Tell her she looks pretty. It will be hard for us to see her in the front of the room of the house everyone crowds into, once the service starts.

They'd never really gone to church, his family. It doesn't really matter to them, our mom says, since they were Indian. Out in the yard, I climbed up high in a tree and looked down on them. Over in his mother's yard, I'd pick muscadines, green grapes, pecans with sandy-colored shells and tar black markings. Some light shells were held inside the harder, darker ones. It depended on the kind of tree. Outside their house, they had an American flag. His father fought in one of the wars, too, the wars they fight in that make them not talk so much anymore, like one day your husband would go off to, and your boys too, three now, if they follow in his footsteps. There will always be a war.

Depending on the season, a new uncle throws a football or a baseball. I get a yellow basket for Easter, yours the pink one. A new girl cousin prances around, showing off her Easter dress. Later, the eggs would be hidden out in the yard, another chance to do good. You must be smart enough to figure out where is the one thing everyone wants, the money egg with one half of its plastic shell silver and the other see-through, coins and bills shaking inside.

We feel more comfortable in the house with our mom. We are not sure yet what all these new people were supposed to mean to us. We fall in and out of fitting in with any number of them.

Sunday was the day once a week that his mother prepared a big meal for everyone over at the house. Once it was time to eat, make your plate, you no longer had to try to play with everyone. Sometimes it was easier to just not try to talk to any of them. Or I try to sit inside at the table in the kitchen where the women do until dinner, while the older men watch TV in the other room. I'm doing well in school. That should be something. Tell them what I'm reading now. At recess I'd get yelled at for sneaking off of the green, over to the cement steps in the shade, trying to bring my book out. The best Christmas present ever would be the one where one of his sisters gets me a couple of books our mom knows I haven't read yet. Mysteries were my favorite. In them you could always know how everything was going to be solved by Chapter XX.

HE ALWAYS HAD DIRT under his fingernails, our stepfather. At work, he banged and ripped them up, slipping with some tool, making the purple blood clot up under his yellow nails, his body's calcium. They'd still keep growing, even after you died. At home, we play with his old first-aid kits, left over from the war. We played in and around all the stacks of old, dirty tires, behind the auto garage where he still works.

During the day, our mom's nightgown would hang up behind the bathroom door, waiting for her that night. We could finger the light blue silk, satin, or something made to feel like that, any time we were in there. The house got quiet, still. Many nights, he was the last one off to bed, finally turning off the TV. He didn't have to get up quite so early for work in the mornings as our mom. I'd stay awake in the bed until I heard him, was sure now he'd gone off to sleep, closing the door to the room he shares with our mom, who has already begun to snore lightly hours before, making that little click, the one she makes with her mouth, while I'm watching the alarm clock.

16

Peeps

SOME VARIETIES ARE PINK, and some are more yellow than anything we've ever seen before. In our new backyard, our stepfather shows us how we can get the nectar inside of the honeysuckle, just a drop or two, pull it out by pulling the stamen of the plant out through the bottom of the blossom, but be careful. You have to go slow. Some are shaped more like bells. Closer to our fence we pick the blackberries and the snake berries, too.

Boys, black, race their shiny BMX dirt bikes around us. I walk the way I do because we are both trying to see who can walk just like the girl on TV, who doesn't drive the General Lee, but a white jeep.

Out in the country they have horses. They have mopeds, too, and all the new boy cousins will take turns. Or they lay their bikes down in the grass, run in and out of the house. One of the uncles has the same name as our real dad. It feels weird at first to go ahead and say it aloud, his name we know but don't use. This uncle was the brother who still lived at home, slept in the den of his parents' house. That was his room in there, where the fireplace was sometimes lit. He'd have no shirt on, and his chest was hairy and skinny. He wore a pair of loose shorts to sleep in, after napping all day, while watching TV, lying on his stomach on the back couch in there, then over onto his back, switching, then going out all night. I'd slipped into his room before, to try to hide, and when he was in there, he asked me something about our new school, so he could say something pointed about what he called all the niggers. He wanted us to know that's what he thought. Yeah, we'd gotten a bigger house, but it was still on that wrong side of town. All the guns in the case in his room were for hunting. He would come down the hall, out of the shower that was at the other end of their house, bath towel wrapped around his now slick body. He came into the den and shut the door behind him. Sometimes he'd invite some of our cousins in, while he was in there, and they'd talk about girls, him saying he'd have to take them out sometime and get them good and drunk. Let him talk to their mothers. He was almost thirty, when he was still living at home. His mom doesn't know what she'd do without him. She'll have to figure it out, once he's married.

His mom used to work in a store that sold everything, to take up some of all the free time she had, while her husband worked on the base, once her kids were all grown up and left, except for the one. On the base, that's where all the jobs are. When Christmas comes, she gives us gift certificates to the store where she used to work, and she always makes sure we have just as many things to open over there as the other kids, when we go over for Christmas Day. Name-brand jeans come from her, our first pair of Lee's. I wear them until the dark blue turns as light as the white of water, until the gold thread of the right pocket gives.

AT RECESS, the ropes at school lash around the girls faster and faster, as they hop up, try to stay in the air, just the right amount of time, rebounding from the ground only, for, just, that one second gravity takes a break, from pulling them back down, as they jump their way back up. We start a new school because we've moved out of the old one's district. Again, we're moving.

It would have been different if I knew how to play basketball already, but I don't, and so I'm too embarrassed to learn to try. I'm okay at running the track, because all it requires is to keep going lap after lap. You could slow down when you wanted, or just walk when you need to. I stop the ropes spinning around, messing all up those who know what they're doing. I have to go back to the end of the line, wait until the next girl enters the field of the spinning, until she can't go no more, and then the next takes a turn, to move the line up.

Sometimes it would take the entire break to get through the line again. It would be this way every day at school, outside for break, then recess, twice a day, before we got to go back to sit at our desks. Unless it was too cold to go outside. Then we'd spend break in the halls of the school.

If it ever got cold enough to snow in Georgia, we'd have to wrap up if we wanted to go out and play in it, and our mom would try to bundle us each up, the best she could, because she didn't want us getting sick. First you, in layer after layer. Till we can barely even see your face. The finishing touch on me would be our stepfather's old, thick coat that practically swallowed me, hanging down to the ground, but that's fine for just the snow. The inside was lined with white lamb's fur, brushed out, and knotted up in the tangles that would keep a body warm.

ONCE, ONE TIME, I was going to be strong enough to hold myself up over the ground. I'm going to be able to make my way across in the air from one tree to another, when boys in the neighborhood had strung a green rubberhose, yellow stripe, taut from one tree high off the ground and across to another's branches. The aim is to make it all the way across, without falling to the ground, hands, arms, pulling you along the length of the hose, getting all the way to the other side before your muscles give out, and once I make it over to the other tree, it is easy to swing up into the cradle of its branches, towards the top, up off the ground.

They wouldn't be able to believe I made it all the way

across, say they never knew I was strong. Then everyone will want to wrestle me, because of that, all want to see if they can beat me. If they got you down on the trampoline, they had to hold you there, until they count to three. Someone slams me down, and I buck under them at two, then lying and staying there for three. The Russian Sickle is to slam into the chest, the neck, across the shoulders, face. An elbow to the nose, just playing. I could taste my tongue, but I was okay. You have to pick a wrestler's name, from TV.

I'm always picked to go up against the same boy, because we are about the same size. The matches took place every day behind his house on his trampoline. Sometimes they started to really fight, to throw real punches, just not to the face, after exhausting a few moves, gestures from TV easily imitated. I don't know any of them, but I am limber enough that it mostly helps me get out of the stock holds, repeated. Am I sure I'm all right, when one of them has done something to really hurt me. I have to go home, then, I say, after I say I'm okay.

I'LL RUN OUT of the house into the street that circles our block, once one of them that come by on their BMXs shows up. There's one of them that doesn't seem more interested in you than me, though in the end, you'd get them all. He's tall, skinny, light skinned, wears a lot of green Levi's. Our mom uses the word lanky to talk about his long body. He'd help me get up on the handlebars of his bike, and then ride around the block with me, until my weight started to get too heavy for him, to keep pedaling, and he starts getting out of breath and tired. He hadn't always lived there in the South. He was from somewhere else. He'd only moved to our neighborhood a year or two ago, because he had to come live with his aunt now. I'd never ask him about his real parents. He'll touch between his legs, say it's rubbing, lift me up to where I can balance on the handlebars, and then he takes off, so the rest of the neighborhood could see us coming, move out of the way. We meet up with the other black boys who had these kinds of bikes, something our mom said it was unnecessary to spend so much money on, who come and go with us.

SOMEONE LIKE HIM would eventually grow up and change his entire identity, so that he might move better among their parties, off at college. They all liked me okay at this time, because of you, my sister. They really liked you. It was obvious, anyone in the yard could see that, but they said it, too. Everyone at school also starts to see it. Tell them all that you're just good friends, that nothing else ever happened. If you were ever going to go around the block, I had to go with you. And some of them would never say anything bad about me, because of you. They won't ask me over to spend the night, though. And we know our mom wouldn't let me spend the night with the black ones, anyway. Your stepfather really wouldn't like that. We know that, and we needed to be careful about these kinds of things. If we stayed out all night like the other kids in our neighborhood, we were just going to get into trouble, though Joseph with his green jeans was polite. He always called our mom by her married name and right title. We could see them before supper, before our stepfather got home.

17

Coach

I AM SURPRISED he seems to like me, a black man, tall, with long, ropey arm and leg muscles. During the week devoted to the President's Physical Fitness Test, everyone has to try to do as many sit-ups as they can in one minute. The requirements to be in shape are different for boys and girls. One boy holds another's feet down. Next was the test of the long jump. Where you landed from the chalked line was marked. Our coach writes it all down on pages filled with lines and boxes, on the clipboard he carries from each station of the test to the next. Tomorrow, we are all going to have to try and do pull-ups. I wouldn't be able to do even one, single pull-up. I'd drop down from the bar. No amount of encouragement would help me pull my chin up past it. How many could I do last year? My tennis shoes will hit the ground. The best moment comes right before I let myself fall, drop down, right before the coach gets on me, before the teasing all around turns uglier. Carter's standard applied across the board, for everyone. I would be found unbelievably pathetic.

Before then, everyone had just been waiting, standing around, waiting for their own turns. Everyone is watching me during mine to see how many I'll be able to do. They all see how I've been becoming what they call his pet. Used to be. They hate that. I was so close to really disappointing him, unless I could get myself up, chin over the bar above my head. He knows I can do at least one, his hand on my back to try and help steady me, palm then just lightly grazing me. Start. He has to pick me up in order for me to be able to grab the bar. I can't just jump up. I'm too short. Then I'm in a cup of his hands, his fingers holding tightly onto either side of me, around my stomach, at my ribcage. He's then letting go of me. He says come on, waiting with the clipboard, while I dangle at the bar. Go.

He also coaches the tumbling team, and I've wanted to try to be on that. It was spring every year, right before the next sport was in season. There were only a couple of weeks for tumbling, but everyone would practice it at recess, and he'd pick the best ones for the school presentation. You practice tucking your body, jumping over the student in front of you on their hands and knees, rolling once you hit the mat.

I've gotten the new tennis shoes I've begged our mom to buy for me on clearance at Belk Mathew's in the mall. Even on sale, she still says we can barely afford them, that they are very expensive. They're lime green with yellow soles and silver buckles, laces black and white checkered.

Our coach calls them my rocker shoes, joking. He says I'm something else.

At school, John Wilson can do the Moonwalk. Whenever our teacher leaves the room, as soon as she does, just for a second, he jumps up. I beg him to do it, again, for me, always, again. She's not coming back yet. John is so talented, I think, really talented. I can tell that he likes the way I like how he moves across the room. I clap loudest. Sometimes I am the only kid clapping.

After tumbling, next is who gets picked for what baseball team. Everyone had to be on a team. I should really try. All you have to do is follow the ball with your eye. I'll try so hard, I'll actually once hit what is pitched at me. Then I manage to make it to first base. After that, when I step up to bat, they all expect the same from me again. All you had to do was get to first. Then I was going to steal second, and I'd manage that, too. They were all so suddenly excited about me, all the boys behind the fence on my team. I decided to make it all the way home, to steal third. Sliding into third, which you shouldn't do, I slip, land down on the ground on my wrist, with my elbow popped out of the socket. Up and down that side of my body, it's all hot. I'm fighting the waves that are washing through my body. They all want to laugh, but they know it must really hurt. Our coach walks me inside, guides me back up close to the doors of the school, to go to the office to call our mom. I could lean into his side, for support, that's fine. Could I walk? He can carry me if I can't walk. That's the same arm I've broken twice already before. If it happened again, it was never going to heal.

KEVIN BROWN WAS one of our first friends, because he lived across from us on Camellia Circle, where the attic ran the entire length of the old house, up where we weren't supposed to go or play. Just his mother alone was raising him. Some days our mom would let us go over across the street with him, if we stayed in the front yard, so she could see us if she looked out the window, see we were still right there. Kevin begs us to come inside and play in his room, and sometimes we'd chance it, figuring our mom wouldn't be looking out at us again for a while. We had some time, and we snuck following after him into his room, later lying we'd been in the yard the whole time. We'd just gone around to the back for a second. We were convenient play-mates. His yard was roped off by a thin, wire fence, rickety it had been jumped so many times, so many times scaled halfway, then pulled down at the top from the weight there the rest of the way. We were always supposed to stay inside the fence, if we were going to be playing in Kevin's back-yard. We could now make the fence bend down this way and that, twist, because we'd been up and down along it so many times. Finally, it would stay so bent down it was easy enough to just step over it.

Kevin ran around in the summer without his shirt on,

but I didn't, embarrassed by my chest. Older boys riding by on their bikes would compare it to a bird, with the bones showing through easily, and because it doesn't have any hair on it. I wanted Kevin and I to start a club. It'd be all ours. I sat on the side of the fence that could now curl under us, support us like a hammock. We hadn't been called in to supper yet. I could balance on the fence, walk from one curled down end up to the other, up towards the top. Let's pretend, I say, the fence is our boat. There were the flowers all around us with their yellow belled shapes. We began to weave them intricately into the fence and among honeysuckle already there growing along it in vines. We could have to live off the nectar. We are close, like the dark inside the shed in his backyard nobody uses. The old shed was made of wood the termites were eating into in places, burrowing into it, gnawing it up into a fine dust that became almost like sand, caught up under our nails. We pulled away chunks of the wood and watched the larval bodies going to work. The doors were so worn down they no longer met correctly. The shed had lots of forgotten junk in it. We slide our thin bodies inside between the space between the doors, where we aren't sup-posed to be, because it was chained. We could still get in this way. Once in the dark, we would just be there together. You could smell the rot of an old mattress, gone brown and yellow, in among the cans of half-used paint. Don't get into that paint. You were there in the dark, because you wanted to play, too, and Kevin would go over to where you were now, take your hand, and you could feel how warm he was. I'd sit there and wait and hold my breath. It was better being here, though, than being at home.

18

House

OUR STEPFATHER strips down to just his white underwear, lies on the couch in his briefs in front of the TV,
turned up loud, so he can hear the announcements,
cheering, scores for another sport I'll never play, during the
heat of the summer in the South, while our mom is away
at work on the weekends, the sun and humidity erasing all
desire to do anything. The air conditioner in the window
is finally turned on, after waiting until the last minute, and
it's too hot to stand it anymore. We walk by him, afraid to
disturb him, because he might by now be snoring, often
the case during these long days. Or he'll be involved some
other way. We'll catch maybe the tail-end of that, or just
the beginning, although I don't completely understand yet
what we are starting to see. We are just told we are
invading his privacy. He doesn't want us in there. He tells
us to get out of the living room. We needed to disappear
for a couple of hours. It grew thicker, the black hair that
curled on his chest, the more down the path towards the
elastic holding up his briefs it went. Sometimes, sleeping

on the couch in his underwear, he would have his hand inside there, eyes closed. He was just pretending to be sleeping, so we'd be quiet. We should leave him alone, go into your room to play. We could come inside the house, out from in the yard, only if we promised to be quiet. Going into the kitchen means we have to walk by him. The washer and dryer were behind a curtain that hung on one side of the room that is your bedroom. On his back, one of his hands stretched up above his head, his length along the cushions of the couch, his lap swims there on the couch. He told us once. Don't bother him. Didn't we hear? The couch would get damp with his sweat.

If we don't want to play in your room, we should go outside. Go play with your sister, when he notices me standing there. I was just getting a glass of water. Why don't we go ride our bikes? In the kitchen, from around the corner of the door, I could keep my eyes on him, try not to move, or make a sound.

PRESSED TOGETHER, our mom's knees would make a support for us, when she was going to clean our ears. Gently, she would put in the Q-tip, move it around, slowly in, slowly out, up near but not too far into the ear canal. Time to change to the other side now. I told her how it felt good. Okay. All done. Over her knee, she'd try to discipline us, too. But never as much as our real dad, who carved a piece of wood, shaped like a long forearm and hand, traced his own to do it, make her a paddle she could use when he was not at home, a piece of wood only about an inch thick. Go cry in your room. When you're done, you can come back out.

We ride our bikes up and down the streets of the new neighborhood. Our stepfather wants us to stay outside, until our mom gets home. We were young still and could imagine we were someone else, somewhere else.

We play like we're twins, but we're separated by one grade at school. We try to come up with a reason why we'll both like, why you're behind. You're the one who's supposed to be so much smarter, the one asked to join FOCUS, that special program. We play like we don't know either of our real parents, like there might be black blood somewhere back in our family. We'd like to believe that, as kids, before it becomes true for your children, and we've already begun to fall in love with the same boys.

We go back into your bedroom, once we feel it is safe to try to slip back into the house again, through the back door, if he hasn't gotten up and locked the screen-door. We tried to not make too much noise opening it. It depends on the day, but one of us always wants to do it more than the other one, back in your bedroom. You want to play like you are Billy's daughter, Christy. I want to be you, because at school, I say it's obvious, Chuck likes you. We say this is why we are doing this, just another couple of hours before our mom will be home. I do what I imagine Chuck would do in the situation, slip down our shorts, to make you happy. We remove ourselves in ways from the immediacy of it. Sometimes in my head I played like I was both you and Chuck, I could feel what Chuck was doing to you, as me. Why do we both like Chuck? Everyone does, his haircut, the comb in his back pocket. Where's Chuck now, the brother of one of your friends. His hair feathered on the side into wings. He was one of the boys at school who could get away with it. That looked good on him.

The one named Jody wants to spend the night with me some time, on some weekend, but our mom doesn't think it would be a good idea. That would mean you and Jody would be in the house together over night. Off and on, he was your boyfriend. She doesn't know if she can trust him. But we've become good friends, me and Jody. He's popular, and he's cute. Everyone wants to sit beside him that year. I'm careful to never touch him, because he might get the wrong idea, though we are friends. He liked it when we were alone together for me to do my impersonations of singers for him. When the woman in the song says dancing, she means something else. I copy them in the videos for him, dancing around in his backyard. He wants to make a tape of me singing, to take to school, to play for everyone. Everyone should get to hear this. On the side of his house, in private, with his tape recorder, I try to do the best version I can for him. But once I hear how I sound, I'll beg him to please give me back the tape, let me erase it.

Don't play it for everyone. But he's going to, before home-room, before the first bell, because it was a deal.

19

Field Trip

THEY ALL LIVED TOGETHER, a bunch of men, there at the fire department we leave school to go visit. They had to, I'm telling you, even sleep there, and I'm thinking now I might be one of them. They had a real Dalmatian, and the pole you slid down, just like you see on TV.

Then splatters of hail, like gravel from the sky, rain down against the windshield of the car. Our mom is yelling at me from the front seat, stop screaming like a little girl. I don't say anything. For the rest of the drive through the rough weather, I sit quietly. She just wants to try to get us home safely, trying to concentrate on driving through this mess. The excitement bursting has been gathering all day now. Once we get home, I go into my room and shut the door. And I wouldn't let you in. I don't want to play with you. Not now.

Before we moved to the new house our stepfather helped us get, we would run outside up and down along the red bricks of the three small apartments that joined to each other in one longer building, A, B, C. C, B, A. We took our crayons out there, to color over the bricks, because we wanted our house to be painted. We colored in the lines of the mortar, filling in that whiteness that sealed the building, there like sand, holding the bricks up on top of each other so they wouldn't fall. We scribbled in our Goldenrod, Dandelion, Feldspar. We defaced this property that wasn't even ours, and our mom was so scared then she screamed. We had to find a way to get off all of those marks. We had no idea what the landlord was likely to do once he saw this, no idea what might happen. He could kick us out of there. She was so scared he was going to take it out on her, somehow.

THE FIRST HOUSE we live in as a new family is bigger than the red brick one, but there is something about this new one we still hate. It comes to feel even less secure. There's more room, but it's always drafty in the winter, when the only source of heat is the radiator in the hall, underground, a grate taking up the middle of the floor that all the bedrooms open out onto. A gas fire burns deep down under the house. You could smell it in the winter, catches you first thing walking in. We can tell, if we go stand over that place where the hole is in the floor, by the blue flame of the pilot light, if it's working. We stand over the vent that blows up and out the heat. We get so cold in that house sometimes we stay close by it, metal heated up under our bare feet. We should step back. It's hot on the metal so it could melt the soles of our shoes. But it doesn't reach all the way through the house.

One night, just like I've been dreaming of it, the house would catch on fire. We are all sleeping in our pajamas, our stepfather in the pair of old gray track shorts he wears to bed, the ones with the elastic around the waist all stretched out. We got clothes from other people, black garbage bags of the old clothes they didn't want anymore. It was new to us, bags stuffed and splitting along some of the seams, full of things other people no longer needed but we could always use.

The night of the fire, our mom pulls us each up out of bed, covers our eyes, one hand over the face of each of us. Just come with her. Don't ask questions. Not now. Or look at the house on fire. Don't look back at the house. You'd just get scared. We'll panic. Don't look back at the hall, where the fire has come up from below the floor and caught onto something, a shoelace, bursting out. You could still hear it moving through the house, even if you couldn't see it. She pushed me and you into the kitchen, down to the other end of the house. Stay here, wait. Don't move. She'd be right back for us. She promises. I don't know why we don't just run out of the house, why we don't go out into the yard, or the street. It's the middle of the night. The fire station is called, just like they teach you to. Our mom was scared, crying, but she keeps moving through the house, to try to check on things, waiting for them to finally come. Tells us to close our eyes, but I see it, still, make out its orange reflection in the glass of one of the framed pictures we have on the wall by the kitchen, before the smoke starts to take over.

GO. A FIRE TRUCK COMES to the street, in front of the huddle of our family. We stand on the side of the house. Once, if we were lucky, if we stood there, we'd see fireflies. Our new cousins had come over to play with us, and they knew things like this. They captured the lights in clapped hands, down under the sound of slaps. It killed them, left a green glow that marked their palms. Look. Whatever was inside, that made them light up, was a wet streak at first, then drier green, like powder. Then the light goes altogether out. Or they wait until they fold their wings, start crawling along the ground, quick, land. Stamp over with their shoe that spot, one twinkling green put out in the night. They drag their shoes back along the cement of the driveway. It makes a smeared glowing line for a second.

He didn't understand, our stepfather, what we found so engrossing about the photo albums in the house, how we'd pore over them from time to time. We held them open between us on our laps, made room for the images to move past us more slowly. One of us would say sometimes wait, turn back. There's one on that page we wanted to see again. We liked the evidence we'd come from somewhere else, been somewhere else. There was some foundation before this ever present moment. We were not just the product of some whim we didn't fully understand.

ON A NORMAL DAY in our backyard, I couldn't throw the real heavy, metal horseshoes very far. They'd land with a dull thud close to me in the grass. Every year at the company picnic for the garage our stepfather worked at there was a contest. I'd woken recently from a dream where he was telling me to my face how he loved me.

To punish us, he would make us sit silently in a chair, separated from each other, in the middle of our rooms, for an hour or two, sometimes three. We weren't allowed to move. He'd tell us when we could get up. We couldn't touch anything in our room, have anything with us in our chair. That was part of the punishment. We could look at the walls or the floor. That was it. You couldn't fall asleep in the chair, either. That was not allowed. If he caught you, he'd come in and wake you up. When you were being punished, what was the point, if you were just going to sleep? Sometimes we had to sit in the chair until at least until eight o'clock, when we could finally just go to bed. Then we could get out of our chairs, to go to bed. We could come eat, but then we had to go back to the chairs in the middle of our rooms. If we'd done something really wrong, we'd have to get up the next day and sit there all day Sunday, too. We were going to sit there and think about what we'd done. If you sit still the whole time, you get to get up quicker, if he hasn't caught you moving. And sometimes I had been influencing you, making you do whatever, it wasn't all your fault. We didn't even know why we were being punished, did we.

God, be a man, he says. He thinks he knows what we should watch when we watch TV. The book he has on his side of the bed, and that's been there for as long as I can remember now, is about Gary Gilmore, someone who really murdered some people. He tells me to go take my bath, while he's watching the news. I hated taking a shower because I didn't like not being able to hear the rest of the house. Sometimes he came in, threw open the door, saying he just wanted to make sure I was really taking a bath, wanted to make sure I was really washing, not just splashing around. He was going to stand there and watch. I couldn't be done yet. He can see there's no soap in the water, he says. What were you doing in your room.

Increasingly, I'm more afraid. Some nights I could hear him snoring, if I listened close enough, if I stayed real still, still enough. I'll stay awake some nights. In the morning, I can hear our mom starting her car, him trying to get you up in your room. I try get up and get dressed before he comes into mine. Wake up. Don't want him to see me lying there still.

If he takes us all out to the movies for my birthday, I'll get to pick the film we all see. But he won't believe the one I want to go to. He can't believe I really liked that. One day you kids were going to have to enter the real world, he tells us. Or one day we were going to see how good we had it with him.

It only took ten seconds to change the toilet paper roll when someone used the last of it. You do it every single time, don't forget. This was just one of the reasons why he would punish me. Another was when I wouldn't take the time to just lift the toilet seat up before I go to the bathroom, when I walk in there in the middle of the night. He can tell I've been in there, he says. He listens for me. Waits for me to come out. Then he goes in there to check. He's just going to stand there and watch me next time, he says. Or he'll come into my room, grab me up out of bed, after I've left, after he hears me in the hall, take me by the arm, march me right back in there. Go again. Show him how I'm supposed to do it.

Your light purple nightgown, some nights in the hall, when all the commotion wakes you. You couldn't sleep, either. He wakes up the whole house. He was holding me by the scruff of my neck, pulling my skin tight. Choking me. Making my shirt come up, so you could see my ribcage. I never go to bed without a shirt on.

He tried to correct you, too. Look at the way you were walking, chest all out in front of you, your ass stuck all out. Stand up straight, he'd yell. He didn't want to see you walking around like you were one of those girls, niggers, in our neighborhood.

EVEN THOUGH HE WAS from the North, our real dad was such a redneck, our mom said. It didn't matter how hot it would get, he would wear nothing but his long jeans, even in the dead of summer.

Now our stepfather was going to punish me. Makes me sit at the desk in my room. The one they found for me for Christmas, an old one some people they knew were getting rid of, going to throw out. He pulls out one of the drawers and takes out one of the spiral notebooks I have for school, tears from the back a hunk of pages, then slams them down on the desk in front of me, telling me I'm going to fill every line, on every sheets, front and back. Before I can get back in bed, I have to finish this. We've been through this before, haven't we. Writing the same thing again and again, to learn, over and over a thousand times. Number them, too. So you can see. My fingers would cramp holding the pen. Being tired was part of it. He doesn't care if it takes all night. Tells me to quit my crying. Eventually, I'll get used to it. He's going to stand there and watch me until I quit crying, start writing.

I better be finished by the time it's time to go to school in the morning. If I finish before then, I can go to bed. I hold up my head with one hand and write with the other. He better not come in and find me in bed. This would teach me to pay attention to what I'm doing in the middle of the night. Next time, I'd look. Our mom would say don't, some nights in frustration with him. I'd only start crying now if I was too tired. Oh, leave him alone. Our mom would get up and say this some nights if she was too tired with him. He knows I was not going to be able to get up in the morning now, she says, and I had school tomorrow.

I've decided I want to live in Australia, while sitting in my room at the desk, where the varnish of the wood top is in places scratched. A couple of the handles that pull out the drawers towards the bottom have come unhinged, and they then hang lop-sided. On the wide-ruled notebook paper, I'd try to start a diary again. It was a rare day when I got past a couple of entries, when I managed to feel like I was able to look at what I'd thought for more than three days, in a row, a whole week, before I balled up that page I'd started for the new day, went back, balled up all the pages from before.

Day after day on the playground, you had to go out and pretend to kick the ball around. We practice our hand-writing, cursive, repeating it over and over, the loops in the exercise book at school, to master. Now I think I can't wait for summer, when I hope all I'll have to do is read whatever I want. At recess, we were not to get as close to the fence as I got, while one or another new car would occasionally roll slowly by. When one of them got a new truck, another had to go and get an even bigger, better one, in my stepfather's family. Soon there would be so many of these new big trucks they'd overrun the patch of dirt driveway at his parents' house. They'd have to start parking them on the grass, up and down the street, whenever we all went over there.

Look. Sometimes a plane flew overhead, on its way out to the big field that was where they'd find the base. Every year they had the Annual Air Show. Everyone would come out and stand in the field together, looking up at the big blue sky, and the gray and white in it that cut a streak across it. They'd block out every other thought, when they flew low enough. The families brought out their lawn chairs and sat there together, as the pilots began, look, writing up there in the sky.

DOWN INTO A DRY RIVERBED we'd go, he and I. My toes sank into the warm drying mud, and up between them, it would ooze again. Take off your shoes, he'd said. I knew what we were supposed to be doing there, what we were looking for, but what I noticed most was he and I alone. He was trying to teach me the things his nephews already knew. How to be a man, he said.

We were looking for crawdads. I don't want to pick one of them up, as they scurry, run around with their bug-eyes on the ends of long stalks. That's what we were going to use as bait. You had to learn how to quit being such a wimp, baby, a sissy. Come on, pick up one of their bleached bodies that struggled in vain to run away, over the mud of the riverbed, the feelers feebly flicking. Their shelled bodies give. They crunch onto the hooks we'll dangle next over the water. In the river green, on the boat rocking, my face turns colors, too, as the boat dips, with each passing wave, the bamboo pole, another present from him for another Christmas, tipping further under.

20

Maroon

WHEN HE FIRST MOVED IN, when I was younger, I knew I shouldn't want to be so close to him. You could see it in the one picture of me with him holding onto me. I shouldn't like it so much. It was no good trying to get away, when he was going to punish you. You were only going to make it worse. He'd never hurt us, our mom kept saying.

In our new, bigger backyard, I would hide towards dusk in the corn I asked him if he'd grow, too, this year in his garden, tall stalks he never thought anything would come from. Look at how tall it'd gotten, the sky around it all black. He didn't want us out there playing in his garden. We'd never be able to eat all of that corn. It would go brown, turn bad, before we got through even half of it.

We are reminded it's his money that partly helped buy the groceries, and I'd sit there at that table, until I've cleaned my plate. I'd sit there all night, if I had to. We're eating the food from his garden, don't forget.

In Science, we have begun studying chromosomes, why things ended up looking the way they did. It was natural for you to want certain things. Inside the jewelry box in your room, a music box too, on your white dresser, a ballerina pops up when you open it. Inside you kept our mom's old earrings. She'd given them to you to play with, before you could even put them in your ear for real. Some were just clip-ons. Once you did get your ears pierced, people could get you earrings then, for your birthday, Christmas. You'd get our mom's old makeup, whatever she didn't use or need anymore, colors she says she can't wear to the hospital, old high-heels, but just for playing around the house in.

The teacher watching us at recess was not going to tell me again I should be playing kick ball with everyone else, over there. In the library, where I've read some of the books twice now, nobody is allowed to say anything. Some books are for girls, the librarian tells me, you can see that by their jackets. We were allowed to go to the library once we'd finished that day's writing exercise. We were learning up to the letter F, so we write bad, dad, cab, our new word fab.

Over at his parents' house too, I try to hide from them all behind the shed, by the fence. We weren't supposed to go around the shed, but I did. You were not to play around the two or three boats his dad kept in the backyard, boats resting up on wooden stakes driven into the ground, one end, the prow, high up in the air, balanced there. We had to be careful back there, if we were running around. Soon it would be dusk, and the mosquitoes were a good excuse to come back in for the night.

IN THE RED BRICK HOUSE, when I was younger, I could crawl across the floor of our mom's closet, up to under her dresses, the tails of the skirts hanging down, feelings to rub your face up against.

The carpet in the new bathroom was baby blue, lighter, like the white-blue of the sky, softer than any other carpet, almost as light as a cotton, the feeling of feathers, when resting there. A little light came in through the crack at the bottom of the door, where it didn't quite meet the floor, a room that was never completely sealed. The rest of the house was so quiet when no one else was there. Everyone kept saying one day I'd shoot up, all at once, you'll see. One day I'd be as tall as you, though each year we looked less and less like we could be twins, with the nail polish on your fingers to match that on your toes.

It was serious, I told you, just as serious as taking a vow, when I told you I could no longer pretend like I was just like you. I couldn't, no matter how much you begged, wanted someone to still play with, no matter what the game was. Or it would never stop. I knew it. I wanted you to help me, if you could. I couldn't act like that anymore. In the past, it had always made playing with you easier. Sometimes you wanted to be the boy, though, and so then I would just have to be the girl. We'd take turns. Sometimes I would only play with you if you would pretend to be one, too, but you didn't like us both playing like we were him, Chuck. That didn't make any sense to you, but I wanted to be underneath him sometimes, too, where you were supposed to be.

I talked like a sissy. It was from talking with you and our mom, just the three of us. I didn't want there ever to be any reason for me to be taken away from you two.

You won't tell me what happened once, when you went into your room with one of the boys from the neighborhood, closed your door, something you don't want to talk to me about.

21

Dissent

WE'D SLIP OUT to the front yard, feeling the grass under our bare feet, watching that dad next door across the street bringing in something from his car.

Our stepfather had friends. They would come over, stay up with him, drinking in the living room. Our mom would sit up with them for a bit, watching whatever they wanted that night on the TV, decide soon enough it wasn't really her place, going off to bed while someone else hit another baseball. Again, they've taken over the front room. We try to stay in our bedrooms until they have all left, but it's hard to outwait some of them. Our stepfather has slowly worked his way up from general mechanic to one of the managers of the garage. He tells us he keeps food on the table for us. We walk around each other, trying to stay out of each other's way, there in the house, and he'll tell us when he's gonna have some of his friends over to watch the game on TV that night, to be prepared. In the refrigerator, there's a six-pack, another and another, when I open it up to check. It doesn't matter what we want to watch on TV. It's his TV, he says, guesses we'll just have to find something else to do that night, other than watch TV. It's too dark outside, so we can't go outside. Our mom doesn't like us going out after supper. This game would be going on all night, and one of them never goes home, stays until the station has even signed off. He's drunk. Our mom says, he's just lonely. There's nothing at home for him. Our stepfather leaves him on the couch, leaves the TV on for him, finally having to go off to bed, to join our mom who left them out there alone hours ago. Rockets glare on the screen, bombs burst, then a red, white, and blue flag flaps across, filling it all up, unfurling, now in close-up for a second. A breeze you could see but couldn't feel moves it.

He comes over in his compact car, comes over to drink with our stepfather. Another game another night. His family is the one that owns the auto garage and parts shop where our stepfather works, says he spends every day slaving away. They're loaded. He has a nice car, a little younger than our stepfather. Doesn't he have a house, our mom has begun to ask. I want to see inside his car. He's coming over every weekend, but our stepfather says leave him alone. Come off it, he'll say to our mom, he'd rather have him drinking over at our house than out at some bar with no way to get home at the end of the night, drunk as we all know he gets.

I slip out into the yard, while the game is still on, hoping he's left the car unlocked. I go through the glove compartment, find his leather wallet, that skin stretched smooth and shiny to the touch, inside condoms he never gets a chance to use. He had a whole house out in the country to himself, a bachelor. I can hear clearly the cheers on the TV. We'll be able to hear him snoring later on the couch, long after we've all gone to bed. I go to sleep touching myself.

Coughs over other voices in the other room, his, his friend, the TV. Hear him clearing his throat, even though the TV is turned up loud. He's going to sit up a little longer and watch just a bit more of the game. I stay still in bed, while he moves into the hall near my door, almost closed all the way, then past it.

I DON'T LIKE OUR STEPFATHER, not particularly. Don't trust him. He would like me to be someone I'm not. They throw darts, out at the company picnic, during an afternoon that lasts forever. Back at home, I've found some old paperbacks in the hall closet, shoved away in there along with other things: baby books, our baptism candles, some older photo albums. I make sure always to put the books back in the hall closet, behind the extra blankets, where I found them. I could only get them out when nobody else was in the house, so I had to wait until our parents were still at work, or until the nights, when for something to do, they'll go for rides around the block. I was too scared to keep any of them hidden somewhere in my bedroom. It was always possible our mom might go looking for them one day and not be able to find them. They'd like to be alone together for a little while, before it got too dark, and then they'd be trapped all night in the house with us. He takes her out with him in the car. They were only going for a ride around the block. They'd be right back. He'll have the car keys in his hand, and she'll go with him out the door, leaving me alone there, when you're at a friend's house, with their brothers who all liked you. I go to rifle through one of those books, some four hundred yellow pages thick, scanning for only details, books they sold at the front of the grocery store, that in their way would tell women what men really want. They were better even than love advice columns in her magazines. Women wrote in wanting to know things like how big their boyfriends' dicks should be. Someone is influencing the way we talk lately. I could remember, if I tried, being in the shower with our father, how he'd look, how big he seemed to me.

Didn't I ever want to spend the night over at any of my friends' houses? Our mom asks because you have started doing this, all the time, with the girls in your class. We were getting to be that age. But I don't want her to know there's nobody. You could see the way I was alone at school, if you saw me. Our stepfather suggests I spend the night over at the house of one of our cousins, the boys related to him. He and our mother would like to have the house to themselves some weekends.

Those cousins would be quarterbacks, linebackers. They played football for the rival high school, once they got a little older. They all lived on the other side of town, where they go to the high school he graduated from, his Alma Mater. Nobody in his family had ever gone to the one we went to. When we were out with them on the boat, one begs to row it in to the dock, once he's killed the engine, as we begin entering the shallows. Another would hold the string of fish from the day, roped together through their gills, on one side of their faces. They'd stay strung down with the anchor, to keep them fresh, and cold, hid from the sun. We should all be closer, but I'd try not to look at them too closely. They don't touch. They've never shown affection in his family that way. The older one with the brown hair was a little stronger. You touch them under blankets in the den or back bedrooms, or you can let them touch you. We weren't related, not really.

Over there, when I spend the night with the older one, I'd be expected to share his single bed. We're two boys, and the thought that we might accidentally touch, that I might accidentally do that to him, go against me in the middle of the night, touch, brush, that he might say something, scares me. He'll know there's something wrong with me. They'll all have their proof then. I sleep on the inside, where I hug up against the wall, and stay awake through most of the night, if not all of it, until the sun started coming up. If I dropped off then, I wouldn't really sleep that deep. I tried to breathe as shallowly as possible. I wanted him to just forget I was there. We watched TV and had popcorn. He fell asleep in no time. In the morning, there's orange juice, his mom tells us. After breakfast, we should go outside and play. Stay out of the street and out of the woods behind the house, stay in the yard.

22

Angel N.

OUR MOM WOULD BE so proud of me, after our school's Valentine's Day dance, for a while. One of the women she works with at the hospital was a chaperone, and she tells our mom all about how I've gotten up on the stage in the middle to sing, how everyone couldn't believe it. Being at the dance alone would no longer matter. I'd no longer need a date. One boy, who'd be friends with us both, helps me down off the stage, and he keeps begging me to get up there again, do it again. Sing another song. Do it for him.

RIGHT BEFORE JUNIOR HIGH, I'd start going to church again for someone else. I'll want to believe, for his sake, and I'll go and sit beside him. Church is important to him. He likes the other people who go there, being there with them, the way they are nice to him all the time, the only Chinese boy at the Baptist church. If there was really someone up there, in the sky above us, one man above all others, knows everything, he knows these things about me, why I'm there. I'd spend the night with the Chinese boy named Angel, so we could get up and go to church together the next morning. Being baptized in his church would be different than how it happens in a Catholic one, where you had no choice, your parents decided. Next Sunday, I'd be saved for him, when they called for those who wanted to be made pure, to come forward to the front of the church.

When I slept over at his house, we pushed the two couches in his living room together, fronts up against each other, so we could sleep down in there. Cushions pushed up around us, we'd sink even lower, falling asleep after wrestling. I told him between the couches it was like we were on a boat. He wants to wrestle again. That's another part of the deal. I promised we could wrestle. He'd like to spend hours doing this. We start by coming at each other from opposite sides of the bed in his uncle's room, standing up on it, trying to throw each other off or down. He and his mom lived with his uncle, who doesn't like me very much. I could tell. Something about me disgusts his uncle. He'll say things about me in Chinese to his nephew, who understands and says something back.

Sweating still from the wrestling, our bodies getting hot rubbing up and off against each other, late at night, we'd then push the two couches in the living room together. In the morning, sometimes he likes to just stand up there and start wrestling again.

We'd cross the street, to walk between the trees, woods there near his house, to shoot the BB gun. Vines here grew along the ground, over and down around flat headstones of Civil War soldiers. Later he'll get the idea to scare me, pretending like he's possessed, trying to make himself look like his eyes have gone glazed over and talking in a deep voice. He'll chase me through the woods with a big knife he's gotten from a drawer in the kitchen. Just playing. He'll show me how to cock the gun, one he had before I got mine, the pulling-back action that does it, spring-loaded. Stands behind me, now it's my turn, tells me aim, tells me when.

I better enjoy this little break being outside, because when we go back into the house, we were going to wrestle. We had to stop earlier, because he really hurt me and saw how close I was to really crying. Barely holding it back, when he slammed his elbow hard into my nose. Our shorts got all tangled up around us, lying on the floor on our bellies in front of the TV, close to focus on what was on the screen. Well past midnight, he asks if I want to go outside, to go for a walk, just around the block, to take our minds off the movie before we went to sleep. At any hour, he could leave his house. His mom worked all weekend, all night. If we wrestle and get all sweaty again, I can take a shower, just be sure not to get his mom's towels all dirty. She'd be coming home late, early in the morning, if she came home at all. Sometimes she wakes us up in the morning, walking in through the living room.

First thing tomorrow morning, we were going to walk up to the mall, to look at the Swatches. I'd been begging our mom for one like his, to start the next school year. She doesn't know the difference between the men's and the girl's watches. Those with the bigger wristbands would slip right off me, little as my wrists are, even fastened as small as they go. But the chance of losing it matters less than its appearance. At night, next to him, that ticking away was his.

23

Dark Shadows

FOR A MONTH OR SO, before I got too brave too often,
there was our younger step-cousin that I spend more time
with, the really skinny one with the hands that shook. He
never knew his dad, either. She was so young when his
mom had him, but we weren't supposed to know all the
details. It's possible this cousin does something like
looking up to me, because I'm older. We'll sleep on the
couch that folds out. He wants to play video games. He
has lots of different ones. In the morning, I want to stay
longer under the white sheet on the fold-out couch. Here
we play a game we call Vampire. Whoever was being the
vampire got to act like they were going to bite the other
person, giving them three bites marking them as other forever, to turn them like yourself. Opening your mouth, your
breath will be hot, warm, slightly wet against his neck just
before the lips clamp down. Just pretend. Don't really bite.
So we suck instead. Sometimes he'd get to do it to me.
There could be baby vampires, too.

He liked to play like he was the baby, who needed to be

fed. He couldn't feed himself, pretended to cry. I would carry him around the house then in my arms. If you were not the vampire, you played like you were asleep, waiting for him to arrive in the night, when he could only come out. You played with us sometimes, too, but you never spent the night. During the day, the vampire hid in one of the sheds we weren't supposed to play in. One day, the full weight of what we were so close to doing would be grasped, if he ever really sat down and thought about it, put two and two together, and one day he wouldn't want to play this anymore, unless it was with you, only if you were going to be there, too. If he's going to bite one of us, he had to bite both of us. A vampire would never not feed on both bodies, if they were both there in the house. He was going to tell his mother. He says he'll go inside, tell the grown-ups how we were trying to make him play, but we laugh, tell him we're just playing. He doesn't have to really do anything he doesn't want to. This was the last time. Just this last time. He comes for the girl who is the one he's picked out of everyone else, a love stronger than the present, like on the TV show. Last night she forgot to lock the French doors. Look how easily they swing open, under his hand, or he could get in by just dissolving through them.

THE TREES IN THE FRONT and back yard dropped their pinecones, roots growing all in and out of the ground, around them, where some nights mist descends, like in the movies. Out back behind the house our bikes stay chained to the water meter, and they'll begin to rust there. I had the key for the lock on my chain with the one to the house, but I've lost the chain. That was the only key to that padlock. And now anyone could just walk into our house, won't even have to break in, if they find the chain with those keys. Now there's something else to worry about. Our mom says she's going to be afraid to go to sleep that night. If the locks aren't forced, the insurance isn't going to cover anything that gets taken. That would be my fault.

Toward the end of summer, our stepfather began turning the garden under, something he did every year when it was almost time to go back to school. The vegetables rot on the vine, cantaloupes and watermelons yellow and brown on the ground. No use picking them. He knows what he's doing. Don't challenge him. Ones still on vines drop from their weight, split open on the ground, before long, if they haven't already in falling, eventually decompose fully. They turn ripe colors first, then go on to others. This makes good fertilizer. Everything will grow better next year.

One day our mom goes to the hospital, taking herself to have a mild operation she doesn't tell us about until later. What she's gone to do is get her tubes tied, that's what it's called. There was no reason to alarm us. She'd asked our stepfather already, and he'd said he didn't want any children of his own, had decided he was never going to want one. If he'd wanted one, she would have given him one. But he already had us to take care of. She's never regretted us, time and again, she feels she has to reminds us.

WHEN THE BROTHERS of your friends, all those boys, begin coming over, I go back inside now. They were here to see you. The washer and dryer were still going, but soon there would be the hot clothes for the empty basket. I lock the door to the bathroom behind me, begin going through the contents of the big closet in there. During the summer, some days after our stepfather had already come home for his lunch break, gone back to work, I go here, too. Nobody knew where you were, half the time. On the bathroom carpet can be like being on the beach, my eyes closed, the world turning outside. It made no difference where I was, the sun behind the window going out, moving behind a cloud. It approaches supper time. My feet touch the blue plastic of the new clothes hamper, the carpet there on my back, the back of my legs, more so even when rubbing them out to the sides, then back in, sunlight pushing, pulsing steady through the window, making for the designs behind my eyes, as I continue back and forth, over the powder blue carpet, a fleece light and warm or like snow, almost like making sand angels on the beach where our grandparents took us once.

THROUGH THE SLATS of the blinds on our front door, I watch the one other white family on our block, with their problem son. The mom has been married once before, and there's something wrong with the second husband. He can barely see out of one eye, so the government helped them get by. Across the street, the kids cussed at their parents right in the front yard. Only one of those four kids was really his daughter. The parents would leave them alone in the house, to go out driving around to do their paper route, the only kind of job the husband could still do, throwing out the papers, while she drove. Still, they had a swimming pool, the only one in the neighborhood or any around us. Their son stayed in the room with the double glass doors that slid open out onto the pool, his room the one originally designed to be a den. The top floor, it's two stories, another anomaly for the houses around there, was left to the girls. We watch the house fall down around them, the screens from the windows lying out in the front yard. Toys of plastic war heroes, soldiers, explorers, and figures of other species crawl across the dirty green carpet of his room, matted-up in places with spills of food and drinks, matted-up like his hair. So much was shoved up under his bed he never made. Sometimes I went over there, if I was really desperate for someone to play with, but mostly I just watched him from across the street, from behind the door and blinds. Sometimes they'd sneak us into the house, even though we weren't supposed to be in there. He'll get to one day drive around in the car his parents used for delivering the papers, after they'd rolled and rubber-banded them, loaded them all up into the back of the car, driving around to throw them out onto lawns, hands and clothes stained newsprint gray. He'd never get his own car.

In the morning, our stepfather sat quietly on the front porch before driving us off to school, drinking his coffee from his black mug, burnt sometimes from being left on for too long, staring out at the day there before him, that house collapsing across from us. Every morning we'd roll off over the gravel of our driveway, squeezed together in the cab of his truck. I sat in the middle, because I was skinnier, I never ate, he would say. My leg touches against his gray work pants, making a scraping inside me, while you sat up against the passenger side door, looking out the window, waiting for us to get there to school finally. Some days we wouldn't say anything to him, wouldn't even, once out, tell him goodbye. Driving, he reached around my knee for the gearshift, moved it back and forth, touching me again with his arm. I would be in a hurry to slam the door of his truck, which he's told us before about. What has he told us? At one point, we must have loved him. Later in life, you would again, once you yourself were a mom, starting to understand him, or he would more you. I know if the feelings inside of me become too excessive, everything will be lost. Once you showed them what you wanted, they could really hurt you, could feel really justified.

I came home from school to do one of my chores, folding our clean clothes. Someone washed them. Someone loaded the dishwasher. It was not asking too much. I didn't want to touch his white briefs, with their big leg holes, the elastic in the waistband popped, stretched-out in places, gray grease that stains and never comes out, even after being washed again and again, on almost every pair. Compared to his, my legs were tiny. His underwear were so big they would swallow you. I'm making a big deal out of folding his underwear, telling our mom how I don't want to touch them. Give them to her, she says. She'll fold them. There were the lingering traces of the grease from the shop, or his hair down around the drain in the bathtub, and any time we had to go in there and shower after him, we tried not to touch it, tried to make a joke about it.

I'm waiting, now, ready. My eyes are wide and open. It's late one night that I imagine I see something in the dark that has come for me. I'm trying to let it know I know it's there. A feeling floats up in the air above my bed, and I go about trying to keep watch over it. I'm waking up from a dream I have where I'm suffocating, down in a coffin of sorts, plain and pine and already under the ground, the black dirt all around. In the dark of my room, shapes take form. I'm craning my head to try to see the door, see whether it's open or not.

If it is late, and we are watching a movie as a family, he

always falls asleep during it. There are the moments when his mouth goes slack, wide open and wet, while still taking in the air, catching it inside the place like a small boned cave, shells of his teeth lined with gradients of silver fillings, marking where all the holes were before, and when he starts snoring, the sound is close to like he is choking on his own tongue.

I always ask our mom to leave the bathroom or hall light on. I fall asleep starting out at that, the stripe of it through the crack, or blue glow that radiates from his leaving the TV on, their voices talking low. What were they going to do about me.

Something wakes me, and then there is the pale green, beside my bed, the body with its arms stretched out, hands upturned, the vision I watch as it ascends, hovers, sickly and wrong glowing, smiling back down with lips twisted up. I try to blink it away, but it doesn't go anywhere, floats there, looking over its shoulder, to quietly mock the cross our mom, always making me keep things in my room, has placed on the wall. What is there rises up slowly, further into the air, to slip out through the ceiling. I begin my cold sweating. In the day, you could see the muscles clearly defined in the stomach of the man nailed up, spray-painted gold, in the tiny loincloth, on the cross. There was nowhere else for it. Our mom's mother gave her that cross, and she wasn't going to just put it in some hall closet. She didn't care how much I complained.

I stay there under the blankets in the middle of the night, not screaming, though I want to, waiting for the morning lights to start coming on, dawn, dark slowly breaking open. More normal movement would come back to our house. Our stepfather is getting into the shower. You next. We had our breakfast, but after a certain point, it doesn't seem like you and I really lived in that house. We'll have to stay there for a little while longer at least, but we are waiting. The yard fills up with more of the boys our stepfather doesn't think should be over there. At school, you'd become the center of the hall. You had what they wanted, and you started seeing them in other places, too, later at night. It was not until I was off at college that there would be a place for boys like me to meet boys like me.

WHAT HAVE THEY TOLD ME about locking my door behind me when I'm in my room? They want to be able to keep an eye on me, our stepfather says, want to be able to see what I'm up to, what I'm doing in there.

He starts randomly flinging it open. We were not supposed to lock the door to the bathroom, either. Just close it. If it's closed, somebody's in there. I don't want to use the same towel as the one he does, when we are supposed to throw one down over the rug to step out on when getting out of the bath or shower, so we won't drip water all over. It's been a while since he's barged in on me. We were supposed to be adults now. As soon as I went into the bathroom, it wasn't long before he began to pace outside the door.

My bedroom had begun to look more like a storage room than anything else. They thought linoleum might be nice on the floor. I couldn't have carpet, because I'd get sick. Dust, dirt, it would settle down into it, builds up. Whatever they didn't want to put anywhere else in the house, they would put in my room, since I had the biggest room, they said. In this new house, they've taken the one at the other end of the hall, away from ours, even if it is smaller. The weights our stepfather lifted would be moved into mine. They'd only take up part of my room, they say. I sleep beside them. After work, he walks down the hall, to come into my room. In the house, his body gets bigger, the veins underneath his skin beginning to bulge. When he gets home, I have to find something else to do, let him use my room. He takes off his shirt, to work out. He wears his shorts with leg holes cut big and wide, that will fall back and up, whenever he raises his legs, like when in the living room he places his bare feet on the coffee table. Try not to look over in his direction, at all you could now see, while he's just relaxing. His hamstrings, thighs, sometimes you can't help but see. Once I leave home, they move his weights out to the shed, in the yard, once he has just stopped lifting them.

24

Histories

I WOULD BE PLAYING one of the bells, a note in a series that would ring up and down, to accompany the solo leads in one song, when our stepfather's mother came to see me in Chorus for our Christmas concert. The Chorus teacher picks the one sound for me, out of a number of others in a box of the bells, their notes designated by single letters. Mine would be C.

In junior high, for Chorus, we go away for our tour. I'll stay in one of the two cabins for boys. The one I get is the one Jack would also sleep in. Some grades above me, he must have been about fifteen or sixteen. Anyone could see how nicely he dressed, like I want to more. He's popular. All the girls like him. At thirteen, I think of him as cute, that's all. I wouldn't be able to stop talking about it when he compliments me in the hall at school once on the pants I'm wearing. Someone was always trying to be his girl-friend. He was too busy with all of them to have too many male friends.

In the dark that night, I wanted to sleep in the bunk

closest to him, Jack. His voice talked all night about the girls we all thought we knew, but we didn't know them like he knew them. I wanted to be able to hear his voice better, more clearly. What came from him he was telling the whole cabin. There were ways to get closer to him. In the middle of the night, he was going to sneak off, over to one of the cabins the girls were staying in. He'd lead the way, and whoever wanted to follow him could. We stay for two nights. The boys all shower together in one of the large bathrooms of the 4-H camp we are using, except for me.

Soon it would be back to the lake again, and our boy cousins would begin concentrating their energies more obviously on you. You start staying around the cabin with our mom, our stepfather's sisters, the girlfriends, the wives. All of our stepfather's brothers had their girlfriends or wives there. The road in stretches where it was paved would be hot against our bare feet, as we walked down to the dock together. Small, dirt roads branch off of the main one, that take us down to where we wade into the water, looking black today, at the places where the boats were launched from and pulled in and tied up. Some cousin pushes me over from behind, just playing, dunking me down under the water, where their white legs stand. They want to race, until our bodies are close to giving out, swim as far out as we can, before we get scared, where we could still feel comfortable, careful not to go too far past where we could no longer touch, if we were to try to stand now, it drops off suddenly, make sure you can get back to the dock in time, before you get too tired to keep swimming. Float.

You could write about going to the lake, when asked to write about what we've done this summer for vacation, when back to school in the fall, when everyone wants to know what we've done. It's not like it was all that exciting, I try to tell our mom, but the longer I went on about it, she'd tell me I needed to grow up.

AT NIGHTS THERE at the lake it got cold, out on the water, very cold even in the dead of summer, with the breeze coming in off the water. I sometimes wished I could still wrap myself up in his big coat, that one lined with lambs' fur, especially when we went sometimes around Christmas, it could be pretty there then, and he brought it. The grit from the day, the dirt road, covers you, your teeth, the clouds the tires kick up from the loose ground, the gravel that spins out under them, as we ride along in the back of his truck. Our mom would keep him company up front, when we were on our way back to the place everyone in his family called the cabin, even though it was just a trailer out in the woods, on a lot of land his parents bought years ago. We go on like this, with our stepfather, when he and our mom want to go to the lake. Summers become his.

We wake in the trailer, around the same time, making

our way to the kitchen area. We were going to go out on the boat, spend all day on the lake, be prepared. He wears fraying denim shorts, cut off and up so high the bottoms of the white pockets show out, jeans the lightest blue they could get, after wash after wash, his thighs and legs through them. Out on the boat in the middle of the lake, the sun burns down into us. Sick with the sun, tired of sitting there, sweating with the orange life vest on, otherwise we couldn't go out in the middle of the lake, one of us might accidentally fall out of the boat, get knocked unconscious, they say. It could save your life. With just the thinnest strip of land still in sight, our stepfather fishes over the side. The orange cork on the end of his line bobs, the bottom of the lake, all slimy.

We mostly keep to ourselves out there, the four of us, unless other people in his family happened to want to come up that weekend, too. At night, when he had other men there with him, they all went out on the boat alone in the middle of the night, with their kerosene lanterns. Why didn't they take me, our mom asks, suggests. Once it's quiet enough, the lake's surface will be almost completely undisturbed, still. You wouldn't believe how still, how quiet. I tell you this because this was something you'd never seen. I don't say anything in the boat, mostly because I don't want them making fun of the way I talk. It would be my job to hold one of the kerosene lanterns, lit, and that was going to be the light, help the boat be guided out. We don't want to scare the fish with the motor, so we have to row. I sit at the front, shine the light out over the water, rocking slowly, with the waves, so small and slight and barely there, by the time they get to us, others miles across the lake have stirred up and sent out, engines cut long ago, so fish might be fooled into thinking they are again all alone, could come back out.

While the women were at home, asleep in the beds, they were going to skinny dip, after they'd finished fishing for the night. They were getting the fish for supper tomorrow. French toast and eggs were for breakfast. I'd dream other things, in the middle of the night, being naked, and with other boys there, too. It was okay, I was dreaming. Anxiety involves the bathroom at school. I never want to go into there, during break, after lunch, when everyone else goes. Form a line, walk up to the urinals or into the stalls, as they become available. I try to ask, once we are back in class, to then go, be excused. Long ago, our grandmother warns all us boys about them, men that wait for you in the public ones. It was one summer, and we had gone to the pool together, all of us, while on a vacation to the North, finally getting to see everyone we never got to see. She's warning our younger cousins, the boy ones, watch out for a certain man everyone knows in town, to never go into the restroom after him, if they see him going in, and they should come right back out, if he came in while they were in there. I know in my gut instantly what she means. Already I'm not small enough still for him to like me. Our stepfather wraps his hands around one of our younger cousins at the pool, a real one, hair, skin, close to ours. The hug of muscles causes this boy to squeal, while he lifts him then high up in the air, over the head, a bird, plane, throwing him playfully out towards the deep end then.

THERE WAS A RUMOR in junior high school that our Chorus teacher had to be gay. Just think about it. Nobody cared if he was married. In our elementary school, everyone said that about the principal, too, like it was as obvious as the way he held his hand when he walked down the hall.

In Miss Chittester's class, I sit in the back, right next to David, stay after to talk to her about not only English, but also what she's done that weekend. She's telling me how she's seeing a married man, this firefighter, then how all Chippendale's have to be gay. During class, David flirts shamelessly with her, in so many words or less, saying how badly he wants to fuck her, the word he'd use himself outside of class, in the halls. Miss Chittester seems flattered. Her class was the only one David cared about, the only one he even came anywhere close to paying any attention in. He paid the attention to her, waiting for every opportunity to point out to her how she's just spoken in a possible double entendre. He could be really smart, if he wanted to be. Then one day he isn't in class anymore, won't be coming back for a while. One of the other teachers sent him off to the alternative school, where kids will have to go when they can't just come to class like normal anymore.

I'd started sitting on what some of the other kids called the black side of the classroom, like you. I sat in a desk beside the sister of one of those boys who wanted you, a big-boned girl, tall for her age. She'd reach over and touch me where the fabric of my jeans bunched up between my legs, Lee's, beginning to wear thinner, saying how I was fine, that word they and we would use to mean attractive, sexy. She turned to a friend to tell her what she just did, touched me how, and how she wanted to do it again. I try to sit so she could easily, letting her hand drop after placing the piece of the candy she snuck from her pocket into mine, her hand dropped back down into my lap.

Detention for talking too much during class involved scrubbing desks after school with Ajax, removing all cuss words and signatures. I'd let somebody else wear my winter coat, with sleeves that zipped out to make it just a vest, a present from another one of our aunts up north, who was working in a nice department store, so she got a big dis-count. She could get such a thing for me for Christmas. Every day at school, all day long, someone else wears my vest. I'd never taken it off at school before, since I got it, no matter how hot it got in the classroom, but our mom can tell I've been letting someone else wear it, by the way it's stained there all around the collar. She says it's ruined. What happened. Look, there in the back, someone's curls, activator, grease, have left an imprint, all along the back of it, marking the collar in spots, impressions of dirty curls, traces, that would never come out.

ALONE ONE DAY in the house, or maybe even he is there, asleep, big body sprawled out the couch, I take a pair of his underwear from the dirty clothes basket in the bathroom, waiting to be washed, take them into my room, up under my shirt, and close the door. I don't lock the door, but in front of the mirror propped up in my room, a mirror smaller than the big one in yours, on the floor, I take off everything. Then I move my fingers up and down my legs thin like toothpicks. I read in a book about a man who puts on women's underclothes, how it made him feel inside, made him hard. But this was different, I was not doing that. The grease-stained cotton pouch puckered in the front. The fly hole can be pulled open. Bring yourself out in front of the mirror, watch the reflection, looking at yourself, only yourself. A palm still dry when I touch myself, when everything stops but the beating of a heart. Nothing bad would now happen to us, because he was different than our dad. Horsey on his knee. His chasing me would make me scream, his eyes brown. Later I'd try on his big boots, left out always on the front porch.

MORE GUNSHOTS in the middle of the night, another bang following another. When he asks us if we heard them last night, he says he's just trying to talk to us. While we're eating our breakfast at the kitchen table, our stepfather's moving around the house, while we're waiting for him to take us to school. I get up from the table, put my cereal bowl in the sink, go out of the room. I couldn't tell you who I was.

In the eighth grade, there was another teacher who didn't last that long. To keep everyone quiet at their desks, he gave the class work to do during the period, while tall, black boys he says used to be students of his came by to visit with him, graduated now, and with all day free. In the History book, he'd assign another set of questions, for after you'd read the chapter, to keep everyone busy while he went out to talk in the hall, in private, with one of those visiting boys. Sometimes, I'd look up and catch them glancing in at me, pointing at me, even. One day he'd call me up to his desk, tell me to have a seat in one of the chairs he had arranged up there in the front, for when he had his visitors, up where they'd talk and whisper quietly. He wanted everyone else bent over their books. I'll be glad when he tells me not to worry about the assignment. I could do it tomorrow. Tomorrow he'll tell me the same thing. If I'm talking to him, I don't have to do the work. He was chaperoning a dance Friday at the community center. I should come. It would be good to see me there.

It would give us a chance to talk about some of things you couldn't talk about in school. My friend T. would be there. He knows we're friends, knows how much I like him. I'll have to beg our parents to let me go. Our stepfather, when he drives me there and sees I'm obviously going to be the only white person around, won't want to leave me there. It's just a dance, I tell him. Tell him he's being prejudiced, for saying this, even noticing this. He should be glad I'm finally wanting to do something, say I don't even think of myself as white, lying.

The History teacher walks out in the parking lot to the truck, just as our stepfather was about to drive off, take me back home, he doesn't care what I say. But they know each other. Our stepfather works on his car. He knows the History teacher, who says he'll keep an eye on me, promises. I'd be fine, leave me there with him.

I'M WALKING AROUND THE BLOCK, the next weekend. I haven't told our parents where I'm going. Around the block, I say. I'd be back before supper. I walk all the way across town, all the way over to the teacher's house. It takes me half of the afternoon, going fast. He'd said I should stop by, sometime, if I was ever over that way. I'll just tell our parents when I got home late that night I'd gotten lost, I tried to take some shortcut that ended up confusing me.

T. might be there. I knew he sometimes went over to the History teacher's house, on the weekends, just to have a place to get away to, when it's just him and his mom in the house. T. had taken up for me, for a long time now, since coming to our school, after wanting to fight me at first. All you had to do to get him on your side was flatter him enough. Then he takes it as his responsibility to keep all the others, and especially the older white ones with their trucks who went to the high school next to us, from popping off their mouths, calling me things there was no way, technically, I could be yet.

I never find the house that day. I think I know which one it might be, but I'm afraid to go up to the porch, just go ahead and ring the doorbell that could be his. He just watched me dance, nothing happened. Some people would call me his pet, but they'd watch who they said it around.

25

T.

LISTENING TO THEIR MUSIC, I feel closer to them. They'd drive by our house, playing it loud. Sometimes they slowed. That's where we lived. Now in the mornings for pep rallies, we gathered, and I tried to stand close by them, chose to be with them. Once the music had started, we tended towards pushing our bodies against each other. Just dancing. None of those white boys would dare say anything to me now, dare have the guts. They knew who to be scared of. They stayed upstairs at break, while we went down, gathering in the halls of the school. That groping was only part of a dance move. We'd chant at and along with each other move something, move something, would make up our own words to the band drums beating. As fiercely as possible, I'd move, pumping, lower body back and forth, in the air, up and down. Sometimes I'd be one of the ones to even lower myself down to the floor, up and down on the ground, like doing something else in the carpeted hallways.

During Spirit Week, the week that would end with the

Friday our school played the other across town in football, the rival, the school of our stepfather and his family, classes ended early for the parading of more drums, as boys in the band beat them, making their way, marching, through the halls. All of the students could now get up out of their desks, go chant along with the cheerleaders. Every day of this week there'd be another pep rally at break, and they'd push me up to the front of them, like to see just how far I was going to dare to take it, in the name of dancing, all, supposedly, up against whomever they pushed up towards the front with me. Sometimes whatever I did worked, and they'd clap and yell, scream louder. Constantly, to prove this was where you belonged, there with them.

During the normal weeks, I read in the morning in the library, watching out for T. to arrive. Some were there as early as us, because the buses brought them. They'd have their own tables in the library, where nobody sat but them. T. put his hand down on the page of the book I had spread out on the table. It might mean something. Could he sit with me? He had homework to finish up. He knew where to find me, every morning, before the bell for homeroom. He was tired, because he had to work late again last night, close. I could afford to buy clothes like those he dressed in, if I got a part-time job. T. wants to give me something, a folded up a piece of paper, note. We were to be quiet in the library. One of the reasons I went there was because nobody was allowed to say anything out loud, or too loud.

The bell rings, and everyone in there picks up their books, gets ready to go off to class. He and I still sit there. We had permission this week to spend homeroom in the library, because we were both supposed to be working on our senior research papers, and we could use the extra time. The halls outside would then get quiet again. What did I do this weekend, he whispers asking. His legs slid out under the table. Nothing. He wants to know if he can trust me, something he really wants to tell me, something he believes he might be able to, nobody else but me. He frames it in a question in another note. Had I ever thought of having sex with a man before? There's one boy in particular he's been thinking this about. If he says anymore, he has to make sure he could trust me. He knows he can trust me, I tell him. Swear, so he'll tell me. Everyone's had the thought, at one time or another, I write on the piece of paper I pass back, under the table. If they said they never had, it had never crossed their minds, they're lying. It's natural, I write.

It's like it's not just me anymore. Under the table, I waited with my hands for him to pass the paper back. He was trusting me, my opinion. Before, he'd ask if I thought he'd gone too far with his hair, when he'd curl it up or have it styled some week. They'd say things behind his back, but he had a certain assurance, like his choices were his. But sometimes it was hard not to laugh, to believe his hair.

He lived alone with his mom in that efficiency apartment. I knew exactly which one and how to get there, walking. One day, I should come over and visit, some day when his mom's not home. I come in, sit down on the couch, ask him where his bedroom is. Down the end of the hall. Alone with him in his house, he looks relaxed, not nervous the least bit. I should just ask him what I want, why I've come. There's a drug store across the street from where he and his mom live. Will he go over there for me and get some condoms? I'll give him money. I felt like I was close to sleeping with somebody. But if I told him who, he says, he might do it for me. Then I say I want to see his room, see where he sleeps. It's a mess. He needs to clean it up. We're stalling for time. Nothing more I can think to say. He had his homework to get done before this friend comes over. So I'll go then, leave him to his home-work.

If anyone ever wanted to fight me, if anyone ever tried to hurt me, just tell him. He would take care of it. He said that a long time ago.

Yes, I said on the piece of paper, I've felt the way he has, sometimes. Yes, me specifically, pieces beginning now to fall into place. I'll know who he means, when he writes the name of one of them, big, muscles. Of course he doesn't write me. I'd just wanted to see what he was going to say, I write back, I've been lying, really there's nobody for me, I'd just written that.

ONE NIGHT AT THE SKATING RINK, just a dark place for kids our age and older to go on the weekends, where we go now, not to skate ever, where they played music, the cousin of one of the boys you were going out with comes up to me. Going to show me how to really dance, pushes his body up against mine. A challenge, and now it's funny all I know are the few moves I know. Can't come up with anything else. He'll swing out at me, as he danced harder, body lashing against me freely up against the wall.

I'd been out in the woods with the boy before, with you and his cousin, where there was a rope swing and everywhere old tires, a small clearing among the trees, behind the house where they all lived. It was true what everyone always thought about me, wasn't it. He spits, on the ground, near me. Tonight he was going to have to hurt me, show me, so they'll all see, see, he's different than me.

I COULDN'T WAIT for that school year to be over. I didn't want to see the way T. looked at me now mornings in the library, wanted to tell everyone what was in the note. It went through the school quickly. I'd say I wasn't going to say anything else, after giving the few hints I gave. He was my friend, I wasn't going to say anything more.

Soon enough, I'd be allowed to drive to school, get a job. Our stepfather would get a car for me from the shop, fix it up. See, he really did care about me. A Camero. It's his car, they'll say, but I get to use it like it was mine. He's the owner. I park the red and gray Camero, with the thick black stripe down its side, the ratchet shifter from before, when it had been used once for real racing, in the senior parking lot. I go to work in an ice cream parlor where I wear a pink rugby shirt, as part of the uniform. Ride around the streets, as it gets darker. I should go home, but I just kept driving, down the streets I know, trying to find somewhere to get lost, but I know them all, looking for something else. The leather in car around the steering wheel got sticky if you didn't really take care of it. I wanted to feel someone resting against me, that's all I wanted. I'd drive and drive, searching for a place to park the car, whenever I felt I just needed to think more.

26

Girls

IN HIGH SCHOOL, everyone knows the Drama teacher has to be gay. He works with a music director, for the spring musicals, who never thinks it's a good idea to give me a lead. Now that we've been officially adopted by our stepfather, our last name no longer begins with Y, and we're no longer always at the end of the line, since nobody's last name begins with Z, not around there, I go with the M students for homeroom. The teacher who gets us does during the day the Art classes, and there's one time he takes me aside to tell me something. You watch. One day I was going to be someone, he says. Every morning I sit next to one of the football players. Even among the M's, we are alphabetized, so he has no choice. Our last name was the same. He likes my Camero. He's short, hairy, but they still think he's sexy, or they say so, the girls.

You go nights with them, to the manmade lake. It's where they'll take you in their cars. You meet them, when saying you're going to spend the night with one of your friends, find some way to slip out of the house. There are marks from the clay, on your white jeans, from that bank out there, on the other side of the hill, out by where they were going to try to put a golf course. Keep trying to find a way to get away. Everybody at school knows everything about you now. Just like they would soon about me. Our mom, our stepfather, they ask you if you want to be known as the slut of the town, pull you back into the house, try to. You keep fighting them.

The first time for me it isn't with someone I'd ever actually call my boyfriend, the one everyone would know about me being with, once it got all over the school. He went to the other high school, a boy I am in a play with over the summer at the community theater, before my senior year, when I'm still afraid to take my pants off. He can feel me through them, but I don't want to take them off. I'll open his. He knows the reason I'm saying I have to go home now is I just don't want him to take off mine. The Camero is parked in the driveway of his parents' house. He begins touching me there, in the front yard, up against the door of the car. For a second, I'll go back inside, for this thing neither one of us has been allowed to feel before, raking the stubble of his face all over me, proof for myself that I've been there, this was a real night that took place, hair soft and brown. What time did I have to be home. It was only a little after midnight. There is still time. This was when we really stop knowing each other. This was when the real distance was created. I'd find something to say to them.

But rehearsal had never gone on this late before. In truth, he embarrasses me.

The biggest mirror in the house ran the length of the double-sided dresser they'd gotten for you from one of his sisters getting rid of her old furniture when getting all new, was part of it. I wanted to go in there. Your nightstand was a square cube, wood painted white with kittens around a ball of yarn on each of the panels. Our stepfather said you'd really fucked up big this time, before hitting you on the side of the head, before they'd send you away for the summer. I was no better, I just couldn't get pregnant. I didn't know what our grandparents up north knew, about why you were coming to visit, staying all summer. You couldn't stop crying. Was it worth it? Our stepfather and our mom both say they hope it was worth it. Keep baiting you. Finally you just withdraw into your room, before saying you wanted to go away. You want to go away to recover, after that part of you dies, the abortion, because you can no longer look at them. You were so stupid, our mom says, you might never be able to have kids again now. The room has been shut since you've been gone. One doll I know rests inside, on top of a bedspread of plaid in pastels, yellow lighter than you normally see, baby pink, the green like sherbet, a doll as pale as milk, a good china one our stepfather's mother got you for a Christmas, her white nightgown threaded with pink lace down its front, broken finger on the left hand, where it hit up against something once that didn't give.

When was the next time he'd get to see me again? Our parents would think we were just friends, but they'd see it, the rest of the cast, in the way he looked at me. I'd spend the night over there many nights that summer. We wrapped ourselves around the first warm thing we found we felt we could finally have.

THE GIRLS WHO let me stand around with them during break, sit by them at lunch, after what happens with T. and I have to get new friends, they were trying to decide if they still wanted me around them, if it mattered to them whether or not it was true, what was being said when school started back, if they'd still accept me. One of them comes up to confront me. She just wants to tell me, because she's my friend, she says, that some people have been saying things about me. Just wants me to know because she cares about me. I know all about her, her stepmother who in the winter wears the mink coat with high heels out to the stadium for the big football game, lips she smokes through, pursed, bright red, as the boys on the field huddle and hike. She likes me, so I'll stand around at the game with her and her daughter. She buys cigarettes, beer, gives rides home to boys who come over. She's looking out for me, just like Paula, another girl, her mom was. Her uncle, Paula would explain, was like me. But they're Jewish. With the way I'd begin running around, thrown out of the house, if I haven't already decided to leave, never come back, it's good to have their two moms to go between. I can have supper with them, sleep over at their houses, if I need to. I tell everyone that boy I was in the play with over the summer, he liked me, came onto me, and because I wouldn't be with him, he was telling everybody what he was now. It doesn't matter what I say, though. Someone will still punch me in the face, by the water fountain, out at the skating rink. I'd have to stop going out there over the weekends.

I'M TELLING A BOY I work with some version of this, sitting in his car with him, in the dark parking lot of the ice cream parlor, closed now. I know they say these things about him, too. He's best friends with the girl I'd gone farthest with, who worked with us also. She'd invite me over after our shifts, out to where just she and her mom lived. She hated her dad, called him names all the time. Being her boyfriend meant starting by sitting on the couch at night, watching TV, eventually getting closer to each other, arms over, around, on top of each other. If I could stretch this out long enough, start kissing close enough to around the time her mom should be getting home from work, I could leave without having to do too much. That would keep me safe for a while.

I'm telling him I just need to talk to him, start crying in his car. Just want him to admit, but he says he can't say he's like me.

27

Strays

THERE WAS ANOTHER boy at the other high school the people I talked to in Drama were always telling me could be my twin. Those who'd seen him before in other plays said we were so alike. Before long he'd be changing schools and coming to ours. That's how Darrin and I first met. He, too, hears a lot about me. We keep a distance from each other, at first, until one day I'll tell him I could give him a ride, in my car, after rehearsal, wherever he needs to go. He himself doesn't have one to drive to school. His dad doesn't work in a garage. Usually, he takes the bus. His dad worked on the base, though he would never tell me what he did exactly. He'd make me want to share everything with him, even the car, before long. His mom was a waitress. He was ashamed of both of them. I want so much to be with someone like me.

We'll start driving around together, looking for the same things in someone else. Wherever he wants to go. Usually it's to one of the parks he's heard about, where he's gathered what goes on, a ways down the highway. I was not really supposed to be leaving town, not in their car, if I'm still at home and can use it. But he says no one would ever know.

At school, we'd have to try to act like we were just normal friends. It was only natural to explore, while you were still young, Darrin says, and I'm wanting to believe he'll grow out of this, soon, soon get tired of this. I want to be with only him. Looking for someone else was only a phase. One night I'm spending the night, like I'm starting to do on Fridays or Saturdays, try to do once every weekend, so Darrin and I could stay out later, driving around, my own curfew midnight on the weekend. In the morning, in his bed, he's the one who starts it between us. We keep our eyes closed. Then it seems easier to face the fact we are kissing each other, might have been afraid to actually see our two bodies there together in his bed, doing what he's trying to find other men to do with, watch what's beginning to happen. Let ourselves start by just feeling it.

We'd have to have an open relationship, if we were going to have one at all, because he still isn't sure what we should be to each other, no matter what we sometimes did. It doesn't have to mean what I think it has to. He knows he wants me to become a Christian, though, says that'll be his mission as my boyfriend, saving me. He wants to be sure we both go to Heaven when we die, even if he's not my boyfriend. It's what worries him the most, that we might then be separated, he says. It's something he brings up to explain why he can't completely commit to only me.

IF I AM STILL AT HOME, as quietly as possible, I will open one of the storm windows in my room, then pull out the rubber that held the screen in, wedging it up and along in one strip with a butter knife from the kitchen. I'd start working on this as soon as I locked the door behind me, slipping out through the opening I made in the screen. Start heading off up the street, by the middle of the night. I'd walk all the way up to the main one, and down this one I'd walk to the other side of town, over to where Darrin lived. I could tell if his parents were still up in the living room by the gold square that would be thrown onto the green front lawn. From the road, I could see his father, walking around the living room. I tried to move in shadows around to the back, up to Darrin's window, whisper his name lowly enough times he'll finally look out and see me.

They said we looked just alike. We certainly talked just alike, like you and I used to. He doesn't want anyone knowing how his brother beats him up, whenever there's a chance, starts a fight anytime they are left alone in the house. He disgusts him. This embarrasses him, like I would eventually you.

Some weekends he had other plans. Some weekends he was going somewhere else. Somebody else was going to take him. He won't say who, nobody I know. I could come over for an hour, but then his ride would be there. He'd be arriving, and I'd have to go.

ONCE, WE ARE BACKSTAGE, when he's decided he wants to be serious about us. Girls who are our friends, who say they understand, just want to watch us kiss, in the dressing room, so they'll have some proof we really are like we say we are. Even though everyone says it, nobody can really believe it. They want to see what it looks like in real life, boys kissing, and so we do it for them. They think Darrin and I might just be acting.

In high school, for Drama, we go away on a tour to Florida to perform sections of our play. Particular note would be taken of all the empty, complimentary lotion packs Darrin and I leave on the table in the hotel room we'll share with one other boy. Nobody else wants to be in our room with us. We signed up for the rooms weeks before, and there are as many as four, five, six boys stuffed into the other ones. The boy that night in ours, in the other bed, first puts his headphones on, then, to pretend he's going immediately to sleep, a pillow over his head. We could turn the light off whenever we wanted. He's making sure we'll think there's no chance he'll possibly hear whatever we might end up doing, wants to make sure we believe he's not the least bit concerned or interested. The next morning at breakfast, though, with all the high school

Drama students there from other states, too, he'd rush in, first thing, to tell everyone what we must have been doing. We must have been up all night. He knows, he heard, and he saw all the empty lotion packs of lotion. He could hear us, even with a pillow over his head, even with his headphones on, he says, says he was afraid to look, but he knows what we had to have been doing. But over and over again, I was only telling Darrin how I loved him, crying, then massaging him, using the lotion, to sleep, let me.

WE WOULD DRIVE AROUND, late at night, nights I was able to sneak the car down the road and away from the house. It makes so much noise starting it, I have to try to quietly, creak open the door, before popping the gear shift up and into neutral, a ratchet-shifter. Then I am just able to push it down, out of the driveway, our street slants down from there, and I can push the Camero far enough away from the small window of our stepfather and mom's bedroom, out of the driveway that went up under it, down to the end of the street, where it might then be safe enough, because far enough away, to risk starting the car, not wake them up. Darrin is already waiting in his yard. We'd drive by the school in the middle of the night, bus ramp quietly deserted. We could go back to his room, he might let me in through the window, in case anyone was still up in the living room, or we could find some place to park the car, just be together in the car.

I was not going to be enough for him, and that's something I should know right away. He wants to drive down the highway, to look for others, more of us, someone, anyone like the two of us. He needs the attention from as many different, new men as possible. One of the reasons he loves the bar he's found, named for a myth, Pegasus. Somebody tried to burn it down once, because we were all going to hell anyway. And another time, somebody just drove up alongside it and opened fire. Nobody was really hurt. I'd been in there, looking for Darrin, one or two nights, when I couldn't find him, though I tried to take in as little as possible.

HE TELLS ME AS MUCH from the beginning, that we have different priorities. We circle around the park he wants us to drive to. Why do I think I love him, so much? There's our prey, some man alone in the middle of the dark, sitting on the front end of his car parked, up on the hood, propped, smoking a dimly glowing cigarette, everything else swallowed by the night. Darrin wants to go up to him. Hi, hi. What's up. Hanging out. The man tells us he lives at home with his mom, still. We'll go around some more after that, first getting this man's number, sometimes his mother goes out of town, but we are looking for others, something else, for another couple of hours or so, before Darrin and I could both expect our moms to be getting up to get ready for work.

Nothing has ever been enough. I know I need too much. I've always needed too much. Don't forget he, our stepfather, didn't come to live with us because of you or me, and he tells us he doesn't give a damn about us, says if it weren't for our mom protecting us, we wouldn't want to see what he would do to us. But you are not there anymore, right now. He wants to make sure I know how I'm not staying there, will have to go off somewhere else, as soon as I graduate. You're out of there. Fights because he's started to suspect things, all true, about me. The evidence is starting to add up, he says. You better start saving your money now. Better not even look at him wrong, he says. Better watch out, walk a fine line.

28

Starring

TO REHEARSE for the spring musical, we have to be there in the auditorium all weekend. Long hours, but they will be rewarding. Two older boys come in from out of town, where they are going to college, to choreograph our show. They've worked with our director before. They were his students, back when they'd once gone to this high school.

One is cuter than the other, but the other one, the one who acts more flamboyant, touches me more openly. To straighten my back, while he's showing me this or that move. He seems to like me, as he smiles at me. Darrin can't stop talking about the other one, driving around after rehearsal. Other kids in the dance number are dismissed one day, and I'm asked to stay, a little longer, only another hour or so, as the choreographers want to show me something else. Darrin is going to have to take the bus home, or wait for me. I was going to be the lead dancer in the opening number, they've decided. I should stand off stage left, then rush in, as the music starts, at the sound of the wind of the tornado. He counts it out for me, my entrance, follow him, just come behind him, follow him in. Closely behind his steps, copy them, moves he makes, working his way across stage. Come closer, he says, so I can really follow each movement exactly. Hand here. Get right up behind him, pretend I'm him. And he'll pretend he's me.

The other choreographer sits in the back of the auditorium, watching us. Now spin, close your eyes, and fall. He'll catch me, promises. Then I'll learn how to land. Then I'll be able to do it, without him, without even thinking about it. It will be second nature. The next day, tomorrow, the dance number will start with me, centered on the stage, opening the play. Everyone else in the number walks in around me. It's important I create a spell that pulls the audience in, step here, step there.

Technically, we aren't seeing each other anymore. But sometimes I still give Darrin a ride wherever he wants to go. We would make out up in the light room, in the auditorium, where we had our Drama class, never used but once or twice a year in the evening for the big shows. We'd thought about the orchestra pit, too, during lunch, when nobody was around, if the theater had been left unlocked.

For our audition, we have to sing on the stage for one minute. I try to open up my heart, as much as I can. I want one of the roles that would have me there every day after school. We aren't talking, even though you are back, living with us again. You stay in your room, when you aren't at school. Over at Darrin's house, we lock the door. If they walk by it, his parents, walking down the hall, and I am in there, and they try it, that's it. He's not allowed to have me over anymore. Once, when I pretend to be staying the night over at his house, we go to stay with an older couple, two guys Darrin knows from the bar or park or mall, somewhere, who want us to stay over one night. Darrin wants to. He likes the younger one, and that was just something I was going to have to get used to. When we show up, the older man doesn't really say anything, just leads the two of us into their living room. For a while, we talk, and then they say they're going to bed, Darrin and I could have the living room. They can make a pallet for us on the floor. We'll hear them moving in their room, in the middle of the night, but it doesn't sound like they're really doing anything, maybe fighting. Darrin gets up repeatedly, to go into the kitchen for water. So does the younger guy. Do we tell each other everything?

There's a thing that happens at home, something else, this scene I couldn't just find myself folding into everything else. They'd told you how you were not going to get your nose pierced. While our mom says she gives up, he's set about trying to hurt us, to try to show us who's still boss. They didn't care, we were going to listen to him, them. One more morning he was taking us to school. I'm at the kitchen table, eating cereal. You're done, you say, getting up to put the bowl in the sink. He walks into the kitchen, what's that on your nose, he wants to know. What. You say something else, trying to get, walk away. Don't fucking lie to him. He grabs you, pushes you up into the corner in the kitchen, up against the sink, his body up against you, like he tried too to make me shrink. Look at him. Into his face, at him. When he's talking to you. Asking you a question. A slap, maybe, before he grabs you by the nose, then, on the place that's been pierced, grabbing you there, between his thumb and forefinger, squeezing your nose shut, you beginning to scream bloody murder, the instant he touched it, until you fall down on the floor, screaming. You took it out, and you were going to put it back in at school.

DARRIN HAS GOTTEN a job as a waiter, at the Officer's Club on the base. One of the guys he waits tables with does drag, down the highway, on the weekend at Pegasus, dressing up like Whitney Houston. There's also a policeman up the street Darrin knows about, living with his boyfriend, Dean. I meet them all in the mall sometimes. Some nights, the policeman and his boyfriend, who say they like my company, invite me to sleep on their couch, when I don't want to go back home, and they offer me their spare room, say it's there for me, anytime I feel like I need a place to stay. I think I really might never go back this time, I'm saying one night to them in their living room, but then the spare room is no longer empty. Dean's sister was moving in with her baby, because she was leaving her husband.

You could see they were a couple just like any other couple. Of the two of them, Dean was the one I thought was handsome. What I hope is that one day I could have what they do, one day live like them. I go over there, when our parents think I'm going to work, or that I'm supposed to be at rehearsal for some play. Dean is out on patrol, and I sit and talk to his boyfriend, who left home when he was fifteen, who asks about our dad, a question I don't know how to answer. I say we don't know anything about him, not really. He must have been handsome, Dean's boyfriend will say. We kept quiet about him in the house, because we knew it would hurt our mom too much, and he'd hurt us. He drank because he didn't want to be with us. We thought for a couple of years maybe one day he'd write. We believed some things, at first, to make ourselves feel better.

Our mom would say, if ever she was forced to comment on him, if he was brought up, he could be dead in a ditch, for all we knew. She'd also say that nobody had ever tried to keep him from us. We don't want to drive her away, too, do we?

I WAS STILL COMING to school for Drama, the only reason I hadn't dropped out yet. But next year the spring musical would be taken over by the boys and girls of Prayer Club, who had decided our stage was the best place for them to spread the message, through the voices God had blessed them with, and because they can sing, they'll all be cast in the leads. Of course I'm just jealous. The choreographers from last year would not be asked back. Being the Tornado in *The Wiz* should have been enough for me. Wasn't it? Our Drama coach sits back in his big, round, comfortable chair.

Darrin was back in one of his church going phases again, too.

None of us were safe from becoming like Stacey, who now believed she'd found the answer to everything, all of life's problems, her past behavior, like you would too, once you start having children. What could life mean, without someone like him in it to take up all of our slack? By that point, she had begun to be rejected by everyone else, all the boys she'd already been with, with stories of where they'd gone, what they'd done. Only God would make it right again.

She begins wearing new sweaters that button up over white blouses, tame pants, a cross that dangles at her chest, between two more hidden now breasts. The baritone of the Prayer Club noticed she'd been crying in the halls of the school. She and he could be boyfriend and girlfriend. The conversion is rapid.

Darrin says he knows what we'd do if we saw each other, and he says now he has to be good, has decided he might like to have a girlfriend, just to see what it might be like. The one he picks is the guidance counselor's daughter, who wears her sweaters just like Stacey and smiles at me. Anything for more attention.

THE FIRST GUY Darrin was ever with wanted me to spend the night, says it will be better than sleeping on the couch at Dean and his boyfriend's house. That couldn't be too comfortable, he says. He's also a waiter at the Officer's Club. That's how he met Darrin, over one of the summers. Call me, he says, if I change my mind about the couch. There's room over at his place. He'll come pick me up in the Mercedes he drives, even though he's only a waiter. He can afford it, because he still lives at home with his mom. His dad didn't live there with them. His mom worked at the hospital, too. He's closer to our mom's age than mine.

We sleep together in that part of the house where he can mostly keep to himself, down in the basement, where I work on an English paper, due tomorrow at the latest. I can work on it while I wait for him to finish his shift. When he gets home, he'll make us dinner, likes having someone to care for, besides just his mom. We eat upstairs at the kitchen table. At night in the basement, he lights candles and carries me from the floor where I'm working on my paper again, up to his big bed. It won't be long that first night I am there before he reaches over, starts touching me, and turns over onto me, after saying the bed was big enough for the both of us. His mom must be able to hear us down there, must know what her son is doing with the boy in the basement, her son making whimpers soft in the bed. She just wanted her son to be happy. The more excited he got, his sounds would shift, become more piggish. I waited only to feel the wetness against my leg, so I could stop aggressively kissing him. Just going to be part of living with him to get past. But I begin believing him, when he said we didn't have to do anything for me to stay there. The morning after the first night I choose not to sleep with him in his bed, he wants to know how long I'm planning on staying. How fast did I think I could find a place? Should start trying to find one.

I called another man I'd met through Darrin, Darrin who would always introduce me to them. Mostly they were guys he was with last weekend or the weekend before. This one lived in the closest city. He'd drive to the address of the house I give him, where I've been staying in the basement. Stand outside, watching for his nice car, BMW, to approach, roll up under the oak limbs that hung low down over the street, shading. Another man Darrin wanted, at one time or another. I slip into the seat, under his hand on my knee, tires tracking the road. Darrin's waiter will find me gone, when he gets home from work.

He takes me to his house, carries me off to the bed, pulling down the covers, sliding me in under his belly. A dog watches us, from across the room, want, buck, my legs spread open with his, more muscular, by far, than mine.

Here, he takes my head in his hands, puts it where he wants it. The dog barks. It would hurt me too much for him to fuck me, he says, but I could him, if I wanted.

He warns me repeatedly that I can't stay there with him. Just for a couple of nights. The weekend. To keep up appearances, for his family, he has a girlfriend, and she'd be coming over. She wouldn't understand if I was there. He's been called one of the most eligible bachelors this city has, because of his family. That's in the papers. He doesn't want them asking a lot of questions. If I have nowhere else I wanted to go, he could drop me off at the mall.

29

The Drive-In

AFTER THE ICE CREAM PARLOR, I'd move onto Sonic, where everyone drove up in their cars to any one of the many speakers positioned outside and ordered. I was a car-hop, but as this was not exactly the heyday of the place, we didn't wear roller skates. I walked out the glass doors with the food, up to their different cars, horns blowing if you take too long, balancing the food on a bright red, plastic tray. Black shorts and a black, half apron to hold the money in, the ends of the apron's long strings hanging down in the back, and brushing against my calves. Another order up. The car belongs to one of the two, a couple, guys, who've just moved down the street from us. Our stepfather called the nice, shiny sports car, red and vintage, this man's toy. You know what they do together. The eyes of everyone I work with watch me trying not to glide too much out, to be so obvious, and then they ask me how big of a tip he gave me, my neighbor. They bet he gave me a lot, huh?

My manager, Sonny, has hired his cousin to help out

around the place, who will keep asking me if I'm a fag. If I like to butt-fuck, or if I like to get butt-fucked, holding my gaze when he says it. Though even women do this in the book in the closet a woman who works with our mom gave her, the stress was still on love. They peg me at work. I could tie a cherry stem with my tongue, like on TV. The short-order cook dings the bell. I take the tray outside, hook it onto the window waiting, snap the change out of the coin belt hooked to my apron. No, keep it. He touches me, pushing my hand back, me smelling like salt, and inside, Sonny's cousin asks me what I'm doing that weekend.

OUR STEPFATHER WALKS BACK calmly to his shed to get the axe. One of the most amazing things that ever actually happens. I've just got back in the Camero from work. Didn't they give me this, the red car with the black racing stripe? A nice car? Did I know how lucky I was, have any idea? He wants an answer. Nothing. Why couldn't I just keep the gas tank off E, just fill it up when it got down to almost empty. All he's asking. Even our mom, not at work now, or back in their room lying down, is there in the front yard with us, you and me, while he begins screaming how he's had it, coming back with the axe from the shed, and raising it high into the air over his head, then striking down, planting it into the front of the Camero, metal entering metal. Wrestles it out and does it again.

Our mom stands there in the yard, screaming, on the front porch with me, while you go back into the house. Almost every day, there was some scenario close to this, but there would never be anything like this again. She's yelling at our stepfather, telling him he's crazy, insane, look at himself. There in the yard still holding the axe. She's calling the police, she says, but she won't. Trying to scare him back to his senses. But he says call them. Up and down the street, the neighbors come to their doors, but all stay behind them, looking out, curious to see what in the world was going on out there. She tells him to put the axe back in the shed.

One day it's this thing, the next him slapping you over and over out there in the yard, chasing you around the back, while you scream now, as loud as you can our business, you don't care if everyone heard, for him to get his hands off of you. He's not touching you. Yells for you to get your ass that instant back in the house, trying to control us. Anytime we went anywhere now in public, there was always someone who was going to say something about me, loud enough for everyone to hear. Even yell it. They don't care if we're there with our mom or not.

It becomes a harder place to navigate, the white boys with their big trucks more prevalent on the weekends, whipped-up to take it out on someone. At the movies, when I try to go one weekend, one walks up to me, says something I don't understand. Then punches at me. Dares me to try to do something.

That night I don't go into the movies. I walk across the highway, where I'll wait until the guy who hit me gets tired of standing around in the parking lot with his friends, waiting to see if I was going to come back around there, waiting until he and his friends got into their cars and trucks finally and drove off.

WHEN WE GO OUT with our mom and our stepfather, you can see it in me. We're going for breakfast, and there's another boy from our school I notice, looking at him like there's possibly more to him.

He graduated the year before. He is sitting alone at one of the tables, like trying to decide something. Possibly, he spent the night at the table in the restaurant that stays open all the time, twenty-four hours, even on Christmas Day. I thought I recognized him.

Our stepfather comes into the bedroom and starts hitting me because I am not going to take anything back. I wasn't going to say this was not who I was. He grabs us, either one of us, whenever one of us would say anything that might set him off. When I called for our mom, called out, yeah, he'd say you better pray, you better pray for her. With the muscles in his arms, straining, he would grab me, tell me I better never think of coming back now, ever, the muscles ripping around me. He doesn't want me talking to anyone in the house, doesn't wanna hear one word coming out of my mouth. Not one. There were things we just wouldn't talk about. If I come back, because I need a place to sleep, have nowhere else to go, I have to agree to his terms.

What happened to my new boyfriend, he'd ask, making his voice go up high. Then telling me to stay in my room. Nobody in that house wants to see my face, close the door. They shouldn't have to see me.

The military, you said, was going to be how you were going to get out of there, thinking you were going to get to see other places, that the world was bigger than anything that could happen in that small, ugly little house. But I couldn't talk to you anymore, either. I resented having been born into this feeling I had to work hard, to figure out how to keep going, get to somewhere where I could finally end up. I couldn't say whether I'd ever see you again. In trying to save himself, I could see how our real dad had left us to fend for ourselves.

ONCE, WHEN OUR STEPFATHER was hurting you, I tried to run out of the house in a moment of panic, run away wherever, upset clearly beyond thinking. Couldn't see the glass screen door in front of me, even. Hit up against it, my body slapping into it, just blindly trying to go. Then I was on the floor, our mom behind me, trying to come over, pick me back up. Saying not you. Not you, too.

When I finally went for good, I don't remember even if you were still there. Where were you. I was trying not to think about what you or our mom might have felt, to go, get out the door. She is lying down on her bed, I remember, crying. Who didn't see this coming. I couldn't stay there any longer, not with him how he was then. But I told her I loved her, it had nothing to do with her. He was her husband. I was going to leave.

I'M CONCENTRATING, in another picture I'm not smiling in, attempting to hold up a bike, my first big one I just got with no training wheels. He helped her get it for me. This was before he made it hard to forget. He's not our real dad. He puts me up on the bicycle. You'd have to wait for your birthday, for your own. I just need to be given a little push to start me going. Then I can go down the street, up to the Stop sign. How could you forget, but that's how one goes on, forgetting you're trying to do it in order to go fast enough to balance. Pedaling without thinking. He lets go, slowly slipping his hand off my back. You'd get it. Don't look back over your shoulder. And down I go, as the hill takes over.

30

The City

IN MY FIRST SCHOOL PICTURE, my Kindergarten class picture, I'm pouting already, with the cowlick in the back that stands straight up. I tell our mom later the reason I look so mad is because the photographer has asked me to say what I don't want to say, trying to make me smile. Football. I couldn't see how I could look so far from what I thought I was.

AS SOON AS WE FINISH school, as soon as we graduate, we try to leave that place behind. The sons, and the daughter, you would go on to have would grow up noticing ones like me more often on the TV, if you didn't monitor so strictly. They had to grow up right, though there's a whole other world out there, something out there that's going to hold onto us. You marry, and then they have no say, can't ever stop you, once you live no longer under their roof. But in the city, I am still just as desperate. Pretend this makes me happy, is what I've always wanted. Weekend nights stretch into weeks. I would yell how this feeling was better than none, when in my desperate love for another boy, our mom would tell me I was sick. On TV, we shoot ourselves, or we find other, colorful ways. When we live together, it will never last. One day you wouldn't know what to say about me, as you keep isolating off bits and pieces.

We were common, dispensable here, mere pennies. Nobody knew the slightest thing about who they looked at. We made sure they didn't. Try to save a little bit of yourself that way.

You could be so alone during the day, inside your head, that sometimes it was like the day never even happened. What you did changed nothing here, as so many faces reflected already on tomorrow.

Curling up to the window, in the middle of the night, I want what I see to be something I know is still miles away. The sky in the dark never stops going. I keep my eyes trained up past other lighted windows, skyscrapers, towers, yellow city, watching for how our moon looks tonight, speck or two of stars, as I'm living across the street from the large, sprawling housing projects, but living here.

THERE ARE SHOTS as often as every other night from across the street, but I sleep still by the window. Gradually, you grow accustomed to them, and the high pitches of the sirens that follow some. Whistles meant someone was coming, warnings. They put a gun in my face one night and tell me I better get the fuck out of there, when they want the money I don't have either, I don't, faggot, I better run, fucking faggot.

One night the shots are six, a bit of a pause between the first and last five, fast, and I can see his form on the steps. Whoever does it has run away. No one to call. No mom wails. One or two ambulances come. Eventually, some police. Before that, nobody touches the boy's body, comes out of the door of the projects.

I keep telling myself I will not die here. I'll find someplace else. Grow up to work in a place like your mom or dad, put on a suit, or go to jail, do someone else's dishes. Or stay, brushing knee up against someone else's in a bar, someone else's device for the night, take me home.

In cartoons, white was the color of the flag that meant you were surrendering. His, our stepfather, was brick, red-brown, used to wipe the excess grease in the shop off his hands. Carrying one around with him at the ready, in the back pocket of his gray pants.

You land right back there near them. They've sold that car, it's junk now, the Camero. Where and how I've gone, while also trying to forget I was ever once there like that.

31

Casualties

AFTER GOING THROUGH the military, after getting married, everything changes for you. One Christmas, you decide to give your husband a baby. Then you follow that one with another one, like a way to undo one night, one operation. Take the first baby boy to go see our grandmother in the North, when she is dying. Steel runs along the sides of the sterile bed, guarding against her falling out in the middle of the night. Slow drip of the liquid that's feeding her entering her, and you sit with the baby beside her bed. There with eyes open. Look, look who you've brought to see her.

Our mom had cried, years ago, though it wasn't her mother dying yet. It was Cathy's, who lived down from us in the brick triplex. We go along with our mom to the funeral home to pay our respects. We don't have to, but we say we'll go with her. We don't want our mom to have to go alone, and we don't want to have to stay at home by ourselves, just for a little bit, when she goes, even though she said she'd only be gone for a second.

Once we got to the funeral home, parked the light blue car outside in the dark, she led us up to the coffin. Told us not to be afraid of death. We stand there with her. She says there was nothing you could do to change the fact that we were all going to have to some day die, while we look at the woman who thought she could help us by taking us to Church, honking outside, on Sunday mornings. They've dressed her in light pink, a gown so light it is almost the color of her skin rouged, in the black shiny coffin. It looks like wax to us, her skin, but she's glowing with her mouth closed, too. I tell our mom, up by her, hands arranged, folded, eyes closed, black hairdo high up on her head on the small white, satin pillow, I want to know what she feels like now. Any minute, it was like she still might sit up. Our mom had lifted us up. Says we could touch if we want. Nobody was looking.

YOU KNOW THIS, that I've already gone earlier to say my goodbyes. Our mom looks around the house at all things her mother gave her, feeling a husband no comfort when something like this happened, when you lost a mother. I'd gone when it would be just me.

I went searching through one of the many shoeboxes in one of the closets in our grandmother's house, a box marked with our mom's name, the first married one scratched out. Inside, I've found a number of pictures of our real dad, am able to see what he looked like, then. In one of them, he is smiling. In another, he is with our grandmother, when she is still young, our mom's age now. Again, smiling. I don't think we ever considered there having been a before, how she must have really liked him at some point. Must have thought he was good for her. I find so many pictures of the two of them, our real dad, our fading grandmother, together, posed. He doesn't look anything like I remembered him, when still close. Then there are the ones of him a little older, with our mom, you, me. You can tell something begins to change, our presence. There we were now. You can see it on his face. Us. Trying not to become resigned, I don't want to go any further than this. Just like I don't want to get any closer than this.

Maybe I will never be ready to say some things in the flesh again. Our stepfather, in the other room, washes up for dinner, water running. There's a flower pattern on the wallpaper in the new house, clovers, green, in bunches. He's gotten the new truck to drive to work, as every Monday morning he would drive us, back to the rock pile, or back to the grind, depending on his mood he'd claim, as we left the house. I remember the dark gray of his work pants near the gearshift, moving inside there, your own knee, his lungs, listening to them rising, falling, filling, falling.

MAYBE YOUR SON pulls on our mom's necklace, catches his hands up next in it, fascinated by it as a lure, moving to the charms on the bracelet on her arm, trying to get the horses there into his mouth. He cries when he wakes up in the middle of the night, in the house in the North, cries when he has a dream he has no way to diminish yet by relating its effect. All he can do for the time being is feel it, then cry out, calling for someone to come, come pick him up.

Pretend there was no reason yet for us to fear anything. Wherever our stepfather was taking us, we didn't yet know. It was just this one winter, in the back of his flatbed, bumping and rocking, us playing like we were already there, to temper excitement.

32

The Base

ONCE WE MOVE SOUTH, in our front yard, there is our real dad's car, broken, white, that has stopped being opened. A tree, with flowers that go brown once they hit the ground, bruise then split, their skins becoming after all mixed and speckled, shades it. Twin girls up the road have dirty red, stringy hair, the porch of their house collapsing gray wood. One of them needed glasses to see. She was a little older than me. Some days I'd rather be alone, than have them come looking for us. The poverty was embarrassing. We've started to know already we weren't going to be different. Every day there, we'd become more like where we were now. The car was parked in the grassy lot across the street because it was the only place there was any room. The vinyl inside, the plastic of the seats, began to split open in the constant beating sun, yellow sponge of cushions now able to be pulled out. I manage to get into the car, to hide, before I notice the ants pouring all over the sticky, clear floor mats. My leg makes a soft sucking sound when I pull it up. Some of them had wings, some still more larval, almost worms. They'd grow legs later. They wouldn't bite you. They weren't the fire ants you were warned constantly about. They'll start crawling on me, while I curl up in the backseat. Try to keep quiet while brushing them off. You or the two boys or the twin girls would never find me. Everyone there lived with their mom. I'm starting to get scared I might be hiding too well, that I'll never be found. All day long, the day gets darker, until it's gone. You'll stop looking.

IT'S THE CLOSE PROXIMITY to our father that I'll remember most, more than his face, his body. I am pretending in the shower it was raining. I try to collect puddles in my cupped hands, while he's in there with me, showering together. We were going to get wet if we didn't hurry up and get out. He washes me for me, and I'd do it for him. My head comes now to just about his bellybutton. I like to turn my back to him, so I won't have to look at things. I try to play with the shampoo bottles, remove myself further off into the corner of the tub, making more space between us, our skins humid in the heat, the hot water down the trail of his chest, when he puts his head under. Our mom and you were waiting to get in. There were four of us in the house. We took turns over who got to go in with who. Tells me to close my eyes, rinsing my hair.

Before we left for the South, our dad still lived with us in a house down the hill from his parents and their field. In the sun, around horses I remember, he works occasionally on a car, light reflecting off a dusted windshield. A project. Over at his parents' house. Dirt gathers on the glass in a fine film, but still mostly it's transparent, beams break through in colors. He wears a white T-shirt, the limbs of his arms, gold, brown. He only works on the car on the weekend, because there's time to repair this engine. His parents had another car he could use. When he plays with us, he would pick us up in his arms and swing us, turning us through the air, making our bodies into planes, jeans flying by our blurred sights. We don't know yet he's just another high school boy, who graduated, then had us.

We are running through the grass, rolling over and down the slight hill just to get dizzy. He takes us aside to show us a trick, the simplest thing, blowing the tips like cotton off, the heads of weeds we call flowers, making them flutter away, scattering easily and dispersing. That's how more flowers were made. But you had to make a wish, too.

The horses would knock you down, if you got too close, if you scared them, if you came up on them wrong. I want to be outside, because I want to be near him. He picks a bit of the white clover flowers, shows us how they're a kind you could eat, if you want.

THE OTHER MEN around our real dad would whisper and point at him, as we walked with him into one of the stores on the base, where he worked on planes. They all stared so intently, I believed. We were two children, red-eyed, not quite sure if we wanted to be holding his hand, so tightly or not. He was going to buy us something, if we came to see him today on the base, where he lived now that the officers made him come away, for hurting our mom again one night in the house.

He couldn't afford the clay I wanted, he said, not with his paycheck, but he told us the price range we could pick something out in. Then the couple of hours we were to spend with him were up. He went to hug us goodbye, when our mom picked us up in his small room at the barracks. You stood against the wall, as far away from him as possible. Looked as though you were not even sure who he was anymore. We had to tell him goodbye now.

THEY PUT HIM IN THE VAN, took him away from the house. But we could go see him there on the base, if we wanted. He was still our dad. Our mom says she was not going to keep us from him, if we wanted to see him, still.

He'd sit sulking and ashamed on the end of his bed in the new room. She would be back in a couple of hours, to pick us up. He looked back and forth between us, me and you, his two kids. First of all, he wanted to apologize. He was sorry for hitting her, for yelling, turning over the kitchen table, breaking the TV. He starts to cry, then. Crying made him ugly. On the cot he was sobering up then. He just wanted to go back home. We had to decide which one of them we wanted to stay with. You were younger than five. We didn't have to see him, our mom reminded us, when I complained about how going there to the base made me feel.

HE WAS SMOKING on what ended up being the last day we visit. Wipe your face on your sleeve. We cried at the beginning or we cried at the end. Sometimes both. He cried to try to show us he was sorry.

He shared his room with another man, another soldier who might be there for the same reason he was. But the other soldier, a black man, isn't around that last day. He wanted to give our dad some time alone with us. None of the other men we saw there would have kids with them. A fence went all the way around the base, enclosing it on all sides. He couldn't leave, not until they were ready to ship him off somewhere else. They thought they knew what he needed. He needed to cool off. Needed to think long and hard about what he'd done, so he won't do it again. If he won't go where they want him to, to make it easy on everyone, they threaten him with turning him over to someone else, other authorities.

But he escapes, returns we imagine to the North, his parents. Back to where he drove us from, he would run, further and further from the spot where we would find ourselves. Gone AWOL, the last he is heard or seen from.

On the base we'd just watched him sit quietly on his cot.

So lonely now, being made aware of who he was, puts his head in his hands. We don't want to go see him anymore, we'd say, when our mom asked, partly wanting to make her happy.

If we ever do want to go, just let her know, if we ever change our minds. But we'd become practiced, good at pretending there was no one there in the first place.

About the Author

DOUGLAS A. MARTIN burst onto the American literary scene in 2000 with his sexy debut novel, *Outline of My Lover*, which would go on to be selected by Colm Tobin as International Book of the Year in the *Times Literary Supplement*. He is also the author of *Branwell*, a novel of the Brontë brother; *They Change the Subject*, a book of stories; *In the Time of Assignments*, a book of poetry; and *Your Body Figured*, an experimental narrative. Born in Virginia in 1973, and raised in Georgia, he now lives in New York City.

About Seven Stories Press

SEVEN STORIES PRESS is an independent book publisher based in New York City, with distribution throughout the United States, Canada, England, and Australia. We publish works of the imagination by such writers as Nelson Algren, Russell Banks, Octavia E. Butler, Ani DiFranco, Assia Djebar, Ariel Dorfman, Coco Fusco, Barry Gifford, Lee Stringer, and Kurt Vonnegut, to name a few, together with political titles by voices of conscience, including the Boston Women's Health Collective, Noam Chomsky, Angela Y. Davis, Human Rights Watch, Derrick Jensen, Ralph Nader, Gary Null, Project Censored, Barbara Seaman, Gary Webb, and Howard Zinn, among many others. Seven Stories Press believes publishers have a special responsibility to defend free speech and human rights, and to celebrate the gifts of the human imagination, wherever we can. For additional information, visit www.sevenstories.com.